About the Author

Born in England in the last century, had a happy but peripatetic
childhood, failed his 11+ exams, and failed to get into Art
School. Worked as a cinema projectionist, trainee surveyor,
cleaner, cutter and packer. Enjoys reading, watching silent films
and doing jigsaws.

The Devil's Foot

A. G. Clayton

The Devil's Foot

Olympia Publishers
London

www.olympiapublishers.com
OLYMPIA PAPERBACK EDITION

Copyright © A. G. Clayton 2025

A CIP catalogue record for this title is
available from the British Library.

ISBN: 978-1-80439-878-4

This is a work of fiction.
Names, characters, places and incidents originate from the writer's
imagination. Any resemblance to actual persons, living or dead, is
purely coincidental.

First Published in 2025

Olympia Publishers
Tallis House
2 Tallis Street
London
ACY JAB

Printed in Great Britain

Chapter 1

They hated him. Even those who admired him hated him. He could see it in the way they sat—legs crossed, arms folded, chins set—but mostly, the hate was in their eyes.

The lecture hall was full. He expected nothing less. As well as the faculty heads, professors and students who occupied the main body of the hall, the press had turned out along with television reporters and their cameras, and they took up most of the aisles and the space in front of the stage. A bank of microphones and mobile phones were arrayed around the lectern, ready to capture his every word.

He recognised the familiar faces sitting in the front row: Geoffrey Stanhope his 'boss' and sometime nemesis, Professor Godfrey Dacre, Earth Sciences, his crutches between his knees, Will Haydon representing the new breed of University Teacher, young, brash, commercially savvy.

Standing in the wings, Julian checked his mobile phone. Just a 'good luck' message from Joan. He turned it off and, looking up noticed, standing to the side, a concerned look on his face, the Junior Minister for Education in the Government, Maurice Bond. They had crossed paths a few times at Westminster. *What was he doing here,* thought Julian?

All waited with frenzied anticipation for another shock pronouncement. And why not? Professor Julian Hawkes was news. His views and opinions, frequently expressed in scientific journals or in his capacity as Scientific Advisor to the

Government, were considered bold, provocative, sometimes outlandish, but always contentious. And always newsworthy.

He recalled the day, thirteen years ago, when he had made his first foray into public speaking. The surroundings were familiar—the large hall, an audience eager for controversy but, in those days, more tolerant of diverse views, the fourth estate in attendance. How tame was his subject then: the need for specialist research into genetic engineering to sustain human survival. A few had walked out, most of his contemporaries had stayed. He was regarded as a renegade, but in the rarefied circles of academia one of their own. How things had changed in those intervening years.

Today, a cold October one, in front of the faculty heads, his contemporaries and the world's press, he was going to deliver another bombshell. As he waited for the clamour to die down, he strode out, bold, confident, ready to provoke.

Gripping the lectern, he waited for the silence that gave him the platform, and control, he desired. He was forty-seven years old, with a mane of golden hair, a small goatee beard, intense blue eyes, and a tanned complexion, acquired on a beach on a private island in the Caribbean, the holiday a 'gift' from a corporate sponsor.

That morning, as he had rehearsed his speech, he had dressed in a favourite dark-blue suit, pink shirt, red tie, and brown brogue shoes which gave him the appearance of someone more fitted to the financial world than to the halls of academia. *Another barb for my enemies to use against me,* he had thought.

He glanced down at his notes on the lectern, then drew himself up to his full imposing height. He had been working on this speech for some time. He knew it would be controversial, knew it would ruffle feathers, but he didn't care. It was time that certain topics, for too long buried by liberal left-wing ideologues and socially minded bureaucrats in Brussels, were brought out into the open and aired again. Especially now as England no longer had a place at Europe's top table.

Something he had learned from his time at Westminster as consultant to the Home Office was to temper unwelcome ideas with, at first, generalities, then platitudes, even humour. And so, he began this time, his mellifluous tone reaching all corners of the vast room. At first his audience were tolerant, some even taken aback by the mild content of his discourse on the obstacles facing molecular biology, the science in which he had made his name. Feeling that he had them engrossed, perhaps even captivated, he increased the stakes, his aquiline features becoming harsher, more vivid.

'...if the human race is to survive then it must engineer itself to a higher plane...'

The first murmurs of discontent, coming from some of his fellow faculty members could be heard.

'With natural resources under pressure to deliver to an ever-expanding world population the need to design the right sort of environment, the right sort of economics, the right sort of people fit enough to inhabit an exceptional elite, is...'

The murmurs became more audible, legs were uncrossed, arms unfolded, chins jutted forward.

He continued brazenly, '...is more pressing than ever. And if we must create an elite to administer and lead a new chapter in humankind then it is time that funds and resources were directed towards that goal. Governments around the world understand the inevitability of social engineering, so why do they deny its validity?'

At this some of the academic staff rose to their feet, one or two turned and, shaking their heads, shuffled out. A group of students who had clearly come prepared for such verbal fireworks advanced to the front of the stage and shouted, 'shame', 'fascist', and other derogatory terms before several burly security men appeared from the wings and pushed them back. The members of the press were having a field-day, feeding off every line, the cameras frantically trying to capture the growing discontent.

Julian went on unperturbed, relishing the disturbance that he had created. 'Because, ladies and gentlemen, of the fear of liberal free-thinking do-gooders with their ideas of equality and fair play. Man was not born equal, nor does he develop and grow of a kind. Genetically every race, every gender, every individual has its own genetic structure that determines its fate.'

More walked out. An angry man wearing a dog collar, Julian recognised the faculty chaplain, strode forward shaking his fist and promising divine retribution. Angry declamations of a more scientific nature resounded around the hall. Julian's fervent demeanour seemed to increase with every condemnation from the auditorium. A few, a very few, discreetly slipped away, perhaps, Julian mused, he had a few supporters amongst the audience.

'In Europe by the time of the Enlightenment men were driving around in carriages, whilst in the African sub- continent, one of the so-called 'cradles of civilisation' the wheel had not even been invented!'

The dam burst. More stood up and stormed angrily out spilling their chairs to the floor. The security men had trouble holding back the students who again rushed the stage. Eggs were thrown, one hitting Julian on his shoulder. One pink-haired young lady almost reached Julian but was seized and hustled violently away.

By now Julian's oratory couldn't be heard above the din.

Reporters were attempting to interview some of the angry members as they made their way to the exit. Others tried to get to Julian for a pithy comment-or-two, but he ignored their appeals, and with the event having been reduced to the likes of a pub brawl, he gathered up his papers and, surrounded by security men, left the stage, but not before he had noticed that Maurice Bond had left too.

Backstage, Julian wiped the remains of the egg from his jacket, thrust the notes of his unfinished speech into his pocket and made his way to the mini cab that was waiting in the courtyard behind the lecture hall.

The car left the University buildings, crossed the river Cam and entered the anonymous suburbs.

A faint smile of satisfaction was tempered by a feeling of frustration at not having delivered the final part of his talk which dealt in detail with an actual experiment he had carried out which he considered would lay the foundations of a serious study of his genetic theory. But he consoled himself with the knowledge that altruism, social cohesion and community were dead in the water. The future, his future, lay ahead, bright and fruitful.

The suburbs were left behind and the flat, open countryside of Cambridgeshire slipped by. A light rain began to fall.

'Would you like some music, sir?' asked the driver in a distinctly foreign accent. Anticipating something modern and ear-splitting Julian declined the offer, settled back, and closed his eyes for the rest of the journey.

Chapter 2

The 'Mendes House' was located in isolation down an unmade single-track road. He had named it after the site in ancient Egypt, which he had visited as a student, where a cult of witchcraft had flourished, and which led to the devil sometimes being referred to as 'the Goat of Mendes'. His wife had not altogether approved but, familiar with his idiosyncrasies, had said nothing. The house, now covered in English Ivy, was a large three-storey structure built in 1920. It had fallen into a state of some disrepair and with the success of his first book on molecular biology Julian had bought it sight unseen.

'Oh, yes,' the estate agent had assured him, 'it's isolated all right. Took me all morning to find it.' Renovations, which were needed, were few and completed whilst he and Joan were abroad after their lightening quick marriage at a registry office in London. Apart from some remedial work on the roof, the main thrust of the improvements centred on his own private laboratory, which had been fitted out with the most up-to-date equipment.

Joan had proved herself a very useful colleague while they were both studying biomedical science at Corpus Christi. Weekends were often spent collecting various species of fruit fly in the countryside around Cambridge for use in experiments.

After he graduated with a Ba-Hons., and eager to have, less a companion and more an assistant, they had eloped. There was little romance about their relationship. Julian already had his sights set on a 'glittering career' as he liked to term the future.

Joan was in awe of him and put up with the occasional bluster and self-promotion secure in the knowledge that he would, one day, succeed.

Her position as wife and man-Friday was curtailed by a car crash in Belgium. After much nagging Julian had let her take the wheel of his Austin-Healey on a quiet section of motorway. But a collision with an articulated lorry, coming at speed off a slip road, had left her paralysed from the waist down. He had been thrown clear and came away with only cuts and bruises. She had remained in hospital in Liege for six weeks. Once he was assured by the doctors that she would survive, albeit with severe disabilities, Julian returned to Cambridge to continue his work. He left visiting to Joan's father, a corpulent and kindly post office manager from Coventry who gave up his job to care for his only child. His opinion of his son-in-law did not trouble Julian and the old man died a few days before Joan returned to England, as if the shock of his only child's condition was too much for him to bear. Joan's mother had died giving birth to her.

For his part, Julian was indifferent to what others thought of him. Guilt was a little-known characteristic in the Julian Hawkes make-up. He considered it a weakness, a wasted emotion—'spilt-milk and all that'—a phrase he often used when defending his position. When Joan finally came home, her bedroom was fitted out with all the latest paraphernalia required for an invalid.

Which was where she lay now as she heard the car draw up on the gravel drive outside. For five years she had been bed-bound despite several failed operations. But they had agreed not to talk about the past, responsibility for the accident having been squarely placed upon the shoulders of the driver of the lorry even though the police investigation had ruled otherwise. It was better for Julian's career that way, she reminded herself.

Julian paid the driver and looked up at the window of his wife's room. He knew he would have to report the day's events to Joan as she took a vicarious delight in his achievements. The sound of the car driving away was replaced by a resounding stillness, then his footsteps on the gravel, the key in the front door and the silence of the hallway. He hesitated, glanced over at the study door, just off the hall, then the corridor that led to the laboratory, but decided that he had better visit his wife first and made his way up the wooden staircase.

Joan had pulled herself up to a sitting position using a pulley system, two large pillows behind her head. The room was simply furnished, functional rather than lavish. On the bedside table were a pack of cards, tissues, a glass of water, her medicines, a small digital radio, a paperback book, and her mobile phone lay on the counterpane beside her.

She looked older than her thirty-four years. Worn down by successive operations, most of them doing little to improve her condition, she had lost her youthful freshness. Her dark hair, already streaked with grey, hung loosely about her shoulders. Her brown eyes lit up as Julian entered.

'Oh, darling. How was it? Why didn't you call me?'

He sat on the bed and took hold of her pale, bony hand.

'It went very well. Did Mrs Crafford come in? Have you taken your pills?'

Mrs Crafford was a local woman who had been a midwife but now came in three times a week to clean and run errands for Joan. She was thorough and efficient but also nosey. Julian had once found her looking around his laboratory, which had led to a new system of locks being installed.

'Of course, she did and of course I did. But tell me all about

14

your speech to the faculty.'

He smiled and patted her hand.

'It went well. Not without its moments, however...'

'Moments?'

'Some of my ideas were not met with the appreciation they merited. But that's to be expected in the world of science, as you know.'

'I know only too well. But, Julian, the article will be published?'

'Of course. No doubt about that. In fact, you must forgive me my dear, I must go down to the study and see if anything has arrived from the publishers.' His patronising manner towards her, rather like a doctor's bedside manner, she had become used to. He stood up and let her hand drop onto the sheet.

'Come up later and we'll play a little whist... like we used to.' She knew her appeal fell on deaf ears. Once he shut the laboratory door behind him it was sometimes hours, even days, before she saw him again.

'Did Mrs Crafford prepare your supper?'

'Of course, you know she always does.'

'I'll bring it up... later.'

'The vicar is calling by this afternoon.' She shot this pointed comment at his back knowing that it would halt his exit. He half-turned in the doorway.

'What time?'

'About three.'

'I'll make sure I'm busy.'

And he was gone. Joan reminded herself of his gift for disappearing at the most inappropriate times, often leaving her to tidy up a tiresome conversation or an awkward moment. His visits always left her feeling inadequate, as if he had not told her everything, that there were secrets…

She picked up her novel, opened it, but found concentration daunting and put it back down again. She turned on the radio, a chamber piece was playing, settled back and closed her eyes, but not before a single tear trickled down her cheek.

Closing the door behind him, at the top of the stairs, Julian hesitated. An uncharacteristic twinge of conscience took him. He did his best for Joan: the finest doctors, the most up-to-date treatment, all paid for privately, but his studies, experiments and writing came first. Briefly he had missed the assistant he had married to allow his work to continue effortlessly but soon found that he could manage without any help. In fact, working alone became an obsession. He only had himself to answer too. Joan begged him to take on someone, a promising student perhaps, and for a short while he considered the prospect. But finding someone who had the right qualities, in particular an awe-inspired devotion to Julian Hawkes, proved impossible.

As soon as he reached the bottom of the stairs he had forgotten about his wife, turned away from the study door and walked purposefully down the corridor leading to his laboratory. He stayed there all afternoon, working, testing. How he loved the clean, white surfaces, the glass test tubes flasks and Petri dishes, the scales, the humidity chamber and the shiny scalpels and surgical instruments.

At five minutes to three o'clock he heard the front door open and close, measured the heavy tread of the vicar on the stairs, and returned to work. It was a disappointment to Julian that Joan had begun to take an interest in religious matters. At Cambridge, when they first met and he had taken her on, he had instilled in her the primacy of science, of facts, of reality. 'Perhaps it was the accident that changed her…' No, he wouldn't go there. Idle speculation was another waste of time along with introspection and self-analysis. How he hated Freud and all his deluded disciples with their gimcrack solutions.

At three forty-five he heard the vicar leave. He worked on for another few hours and almost forgot Joan's supper. He went into the kitchen and took the tray up to her. After promising to play cards when she had finished her meal he went back downstairs and entered his study.

The room was wood panelled with a desk, on which sat a computer. Countless books and journals occupied the shelves that lined the room and the floor. In one corner was a fax machine, next to it a small digital television. On the wall above the desk was an oil painting, 'The Alchemist' by an obscure Flemish artist, Jan de Smet. He stood before the painting, leaned forward, his eyes taking in the details, by now so familiar to him. The rough cavernous room with its clutter of desks and benches, the arcane apparatus, alembics, pots and jugs, pestle and mortar, vials containing strange ores and minerals, larger vessels with body parts, animal and human, pressed against the sides as if desperate to get free. There was a fire in one corner attended by a simple-looking rustic and by the window, sitting at his desk, the Alchemist himself, an old man with long grey beard, studying a giant tome... The painting was a source of inspiration as well as consolation for Julian.

Since becoming disillusioned with his studies at Cambridge he had applied for, and been granted, a year of study at Gottingen University and one day whilst wandering the ancient German town he had come across the antique shop, entered, saw the painting, and bought it. He didn't even barter, much to the owner's surprise, but paid the full price.

As Julian gazed at the picture he recalled with affection his old tutor, Professor Josef Meinengen, who had introduced him to genetics. Meinengen rarely talked about his time at university studying under Professor Steiner who was later put on trial for conducting unethical experiments at a concentration camp in Poland during the war. Julian worked out that Meinengen must have learned about the darker side of genetic theory from his teacher, and he found that he was more than receptive to the knowledge passed on.

The fax machine bursting into life interrupted his reverie. He ripped out the paper and read, with mounting anger, the contents. It was from the Head of the Natural Science Faculty, Geoffrey Stanhope, last seen sitting stony-faced in the audience that morning. *'… it is with regret that we, the board, feel it necessary, because of your radical and incendiary views, to suspend you indefinitely from your post, effective on receipt of this communication…'*

At the bottom of the page; *'NB: Should you wish to discuss the matter after you have had time to reflect, my door is always open.'*

He screwed up the fax and hurled it into the waste bin.

'Idiots… morons… I'll show them, my work will prove them all wrong…' and he stormed out and returned to the laboratory, worked on until, at three in the morning, he tumbled into bed. He didn't disturb Joan although he could see that a light came from under her door.

The next morning, after taking Joan her breakfast, it was the only meal he prepared for her, he visited the study and turned on the television. He was still unsettled over the fax but decided not to inform Joan, not yet anyway, although she could sense that something was troubling him.

The television was permanently tuned to the BBC news

channel, he had no time for other diversions. A familiar round, red-faced politician appeared, and it was only after a few moments that Julian realised that he was the subject of the man's rant.

'It's a bloody disgrace that taxpayer's money is being used to promote bigoted racist theories masquerading as scientific progress. These xenophobic convictions have no place in a parliamentary democracy like ours. Professor 'awkes spouts views that, let's face it, would have been more at home in Nazi Germany…'

The hint of a smile appeared around Julian's lips. He relished criticism if only to bolster his belief in the inviolability of his theories. But he didn't remember seeing the Honourable Member from 'somewhere-up-north' in yesterday's audience… obviously the press had reported the affair.

Then it occurred to him that his position as Scientific Advisor to the Government might come into question. He left the study and went outside to get the morning's papers from the post box by the front gate. Just as he strode across the gravel drive the first car came up the lane closely followed by an outside-broadcast van.

Reporters piled out, some still eating their bacon rolls and pastries, disposable coffee cups in hand. Cameras were set up, mobile phones prepared, in anticipation.

'Professor Hawkes, would you care to comment on this morning's headlines?' came the first question. He was flattered by the attention but, this morning, he had other things on his mind. Anxious that he may have lost the initiative Julian ignored the barrage. He took the two newspapers from the mailbox by the five-bar front gate, his copy of the Daily Telegraph and Joan's Guardian and opened his up. There it was, sharing the front page with a report on the ongoing Middle East Crisis, *'Senior Government Advisor Controversy'*. He opened the Guardian. *'Professor Julian Hawkes Under Pressure to Quit Post'*.

'Are you going to quit, Professor Hawkes, or are you going to let them fire you?'

'What about your position at the University?'

He turned his back on the reporters and was about to return to the house when a voice called out. It was a rather flustered Mrs Crafford, wheeling her bicycle, trying to get through the clamorous throng.

'What's it like working for the Professor?'

Julian opened the gate for her and together they hurried across the drive. The questions continued until the front door was closed behind them.

'Those awful people,' said Mrs Crafford as she parked her bike in the hall and hurried upstairs. Julian left the copy of The Guardian on the hall dresser and returned to his study. As he entered his mobile vibrated in his pocket. It was another reporter asking for an 'exclusive' interview. He cut her off, then noticed a text message. It was from Alice, *'Who's been a naughty boy then?'* He became angrier and deleted the message. He had told her never to contact him unless it was an emergency.

The television was still on. A vaguely familiar student was being interviewed outside the Cavendish Building. '... Total shock and surprise. I had no idea... No, I wasn't actually in one of his classes...' Another student, 'His lectures were always packed, you know? Entertaining...' The reporter interrupted her, 'But what about the Professor's controversial opinions?' She hurried away. The scene switched to the entrance to Corpus Christi College where an elderly Professor, leaning on his crutches, whom Julian recognised as Professor Dacre of Earth

Sciences, was asked for his views. 'Yes, I knew him, of course, we sat on the same ethics committee... a brilliant mind, if a little, how shall I put it... racy?'

'Racy...?' Is that the best they can do, mused Julian. He switched off the set, sat at his desk, turned on the computer and began typing a vociferous statement to his critics.

Joan was solicitous. 'Poor Julian. Why do they write such terrible things about you?' The Guardian was spread out on the bed beside her.

'What are you going to do?' Joan asked. He had told her about Stanhope's fax.

'I've prepared a statement. I'm going to email it to the University, the Press, and the world. It's time I went my own way. Now don't worry. We talked about this before...' He hesitated.

She took his hand. 'I know. And I know that whatever happens you will do what is best... for both of us.' He kissed her and went downstairs.

Mrs Crafford was at the window by the front door. She had her hat and coat on. 'They're still out there and I've got my shopping to do.'

'Would you mind staying for a bit, Mrs Crafford? Do the shopping later.' She reluctantly retired to the kitchen. He opened the front door and strode out.

As Julian approached the gate, the questions came thick and fast. He held up his right hand and an uneasy quiet descended. 'Ladies and gentlemen of the fourth estate... Please... I have prepared a statement which I will shortly communicate to the world. I will answer no more questions.'

There was a stunned silence. Julian turned and walked confidently back to the house. A few more hurried questions were aimed at his back before the inevitable scrabble of feet, slamming of car doors and vehicles starting up and reversing down the lane.

An hour later, from the study window, Julian watched Mrs Crafford open the gate and cycle away towards the village. All was still again. A flock of starlings flew down to finish off the last crumbs of the reporter's breakfast.

He had been busy since the morning's events and a quiet confidence replaced his earlier anger. He had already e-mailed and faxed the University, Home Office and selected newspapers with his statement and formal resignation. He was unhappy that the article based on his lecture, 'Genetics for the Next Generation', would not be published in 'Science Today', a journal which had gladly accepted earlier work. After today, he told himself, they would be queueing up to commission him. He was, once again, master of his own destiny.

Unbeknownst to everyone, even to his wife, Julian had accepted a post with a Swiss Drug Company, the Davos Foundation, based in Zurich, to carry on a program of pure research. The contact had been made a year earlier, the interview had gone well and on the following Monday he was to start work at a newly built facility located in the countryside fifteen miles away from the 'Mendes House'. The laboratory had been designed by him, the equipment especially chosen by him, and he had fought for and obtained a budget far greater than the public sector could offer.

The only small concern that Julian had was that the parent company of Davos was a hi-tech Corporation based in California with other enterprises, many nonmedical, under its wing. His dealings had been with Doctor Stephen Speelman and his associates who had assured him that they were independent and self-governing. Julian was not altogether convinced but because his experiences to date were of constant interference from civil servants and academics, he was persuaded that he was making the right decision. The one element of the deal with Davos that he had insisted on was that there were to be 'no questions asked' about his work. He was free to follow whatever line of research he wanted, free to experiment in any way he felt fit, and he only had to report his findings to the board when it suited him. There had been a few eyebrows raised when he demanded that these conditions be written into his contract, but his persuasive manner and forbidding reputation held the day and they acquiesced to all his demands.

He sat in his study, congratulating himself on his timing and general handling of events. As the weak afternoon sun struggled through the only window he awaited the inevitable plethora of messages, phone calls and e-mails that his resignation was bound to bring. The television news had made a perfunctory statement, the newspapers wouldn't report until the next day, although there would be something in the evening papers. He checked his in-box; nothing yet. There were no messages on the house phone and nothing on his mobile. *Strange,* he thought to himself. *I can't have been forgotten so soon?*

That evening he sat with Joan, and they played a few hands of whist. She won every time.

'Oh, Julian, you are hopeless.' She laughed and began to shuffle the cards, but he stayed her hand and took on a grave expression.

'I know that look, husband. You've got some bad news to tell.'

'Not bad news, wife.' The formality was kindly, without patronisation, a shorthand they often used as if to cement the bonds that held them together. 'But... news that is going to change our lives.' And he confided in her the happenings of the past few days, his new position and what it would mean to her, the most up-to-date medical care, the finest doctors.

'And what will it mean to you?' she asked cannily. Joan knew it wasn't guilt that moved him. He had always justified his actions in benefits for her, for society, for science, never for himself.

'A chance to do the work I've always wanted to do. The kind of work we used to talk of doing but that they wouldn't let me.'

Chapter 3

It was dark and late by the time Julian left the 'Mendes House'. Luckily, there were no reporters at the gate. *Word of his resignations must have filtered through the portals of power by now,* he thought. He swung his sports car down the lane, onto the village road and on towards the motorway.

Two hours later he parked his car in a quiet Belgravia square and walked a short distance under the overhanging trees before turning into a cobbled mews. He stopped outside the doorway of number 7B and looked up at the first-floor window. All was in darkness, and he let himself in with his latchkey. The flat was dark and empty. Julian poured himself a glass of whisky, sat down in the leather armchair and waited. He glanced at his wristwatch, one a.m.

Half-an-hour later a car drew up outside. He heard the slam of a car door, the front door open and close and footsteps up the stairs. A woman entered, took off her coat, flung it on a chair along with her purse and turned on the light. 'Oh, Julian...' She took a step back. 'You startled me.'

She was a little older than Julian, blonde with dark streaks, high cheek bones and piercing blue eyes. She wore a black evening dress, high-heel shoes, and a string of pearls around her neck.

He finished his whisky. 'Out having fun?'

'This is a surprise, Julian. I wasn't expecting you until Thursday.'

He stood up, walked over, and kissed her full on the lips.

'You know me, Alice, impetuous and unpredictable.'

'If I didn't know that I might think you were checking up on me.'

Their relationship had begun as a primarily sexual one but tenderness, respect and a deep bond had grown. Lately though, Alice had noticed that Julian had become tense and sometimes violent towards her. He knew that the arrangement was perilous, not only to his career and to his private life, but he was not averse to a certain amount of trouble. And he was prepared to take risks, for he had long-term plans which involved his mistress.

Alice, for her part, had vowed to be discreet and assume a low-profile existence which, by and large, she had maintained despite several tempting offers. Her loyalty, however, to Julian was total. Never once had she mentioned his name or referred to her knowing him.

'I never know when you're going to turn up. You can't expect me to hang around every night, waiting.' Her accent no longer betrayed her origins in Hoxton, one of six children to a market trader and his alcoholic wife. As a student and by way of an experiment, Julian had spent a delirious night with her in a seedy hotel room in Soho. Nine years later, after a certain amount of notoriety had been bestowed upon him, they met again, quite by chance, at a fund-raising event for the victims of domestic abuse. She had suffered at the hands of her husband and pimp, now in prison after a drug-related killing. Alice had become, by then, more mature, and very desirable.

Their relationship took off again and, needing a London base, Julian had installed her in the Belgravia flat with the strict mandate that, in return for a life of comfort and security, she was to give up her old life and make herself available only to him. She had agreed, persuaded as much by Julian's allure as by the monthly cheques and the luxurious surroundings.

'I was out with a girlfriend. I haven't taken my vows, I'm not a nun,' she explained.

He calmed down, eventually apologised and after a few drinks they went to bed together. He felt no guilt. Joan's disability had put an end to any intimacy, and he was a man not an island.

At four in the morning, he got up and started to put on his clothes. As quietly as he dressed, Alice woke. Still sleepy she sat up and regarded him with a look of disappointment.

'Why do you always have to dash off, Jules?'

'It's what lovers do,' he replied glibly.

'That's no answer.'

'All right then. Because I'm a busy man.'

She had followed his career in the newspapers and on the television and was immensely proud of his achievements, the only downside for her was the knowledge that it was his wife he always returned to.

Julian had reached the bedroom door. Reluctant to see him go she called out, 'But you could stay until the morning.'

'Next time. Thursday. I promise.' His facile reply angered her, and she blurted out… 'You've promised so much since your wife…' She stopped herself, immediately regretting her outburst.

Julian hesitated, turned and stiff with rage he strode back, grabbed her by the shoulders, shook her and threw her back onto the bed.

'I'm sorry, Jules. I…' and she buried her face in the pillow.

'And no more stupid text messages', he shouted out. The bedroom door slammed shut, shortly followed by the downstairs front door. Alice recovered with the help of a glass of wine and sat up in bed wondering where her life was taking her. She loved

Julian but… and she hadn't been out with a girlfriend but a Dutch businessman she had met at the jewellery counter in Harrods that morning. 'Well, Julian leads a double life. Why shouldn't I,' was how she consoled herself.

Early next morning a scrum of reporters and television cameras were once again positioned outside the gate to the 'Mendes House'. All day they were to be disappointed. The only evidence of Professor Julian Hawkes was his sports car parked askew on the gravel drive.

Chapter 4

Julian Taylor Hawkes had an older brother, Hugo, born twenty-two minutes before him. The 'twins' had been a difficult birth, but it wasn't until Hugo was six months old that his mother noticed his lack of reaction to loud sounds. A doctor informed Joyce that he was partially deaf but would probable grow out of it. She also gradually became aware that Hugo seemed indifferent to his surroundings, to his younger brother, to any new noises and smells around the house. He would sit on the floor and play incessantly with the same toy, a small model car, turning it over and over in his hands until the paint began to rub off.

She telephoned her husband, Frank, away on oil business in the Middle East, but all the advice he could give was '…take him to the doctor'. After numerous tests it was determined that Hugo was 'slow', 'dull-witted', a condition unconnected to his deafness. She took him home and wrapped him in cotton wool against the life struggles that he would have to face—and that she would have to face.

A further concern was Julian—was he all right? For a few anxious weeks she kept a keen eye on him, and it was only after dropping a tray of glasses on the floor, and the babies' vocal response to the loud crash, that she began to relax. Julian was all right, in fact he was more than all right. He was sitting up at six months, crawling at ten and teetering around the garden at a year old. The interest he took in anything, and everything was remarkable. It was clear, by the time of their second birthday, that

Julian was far in advance, intellectually, physically, and emotionally, of his older brother.

Joyce often referred to them as her 'divine babies' and gave them the nicknames 'Nut' and 'Geb'. Joyce had studied Egyptology at University and her sons seemed, to her, to be avatars of the divine twins. 'Nut' was Hugo, Goddess of the sky and Julian was 'Geb', God of the earth.

It was while she was taking part on an archaeological dig at Luxor that she and Frank had met. He was a highflier in oil exploration, and they had married quickly when she fell pregnant. Frank had her shipped back to England and a large cold house on the outskirts of Leeds. 'If it's a boy, he'll be able to play for Yorkshire,' he explained. It was only a few years later that she found out that the real reason for his hasty action was a mistress in Cairo who threatened suicide if he left her.

The boys' father was absent for both deliveries and when he did come home, albeit briefly, he hardly acknowledged their existence. He drank heavily and only stayed long enough to settle a few outstanding debts and spend long evenings at the local cricket club in Headingly with a few of his old cronies. Joyce dreaded him staggering back late at night and forcing himself on her.

It was a shock, but not a surprise, when she came home one day to find him hanging from a beam in the garage. He had lost his job a few months earlier and had taken to spending most of his time at the local bookies, without, she found out later, much success. Julian, five years old, on seeing his father suspended in that odd way, and understanding that something was not right, had tried to pull him down. Hugo, thinking it was a game, joined in.

Joyce never really recovered. She did her best for her boys, moved back down south and took whatever work she could find to pay the rent on a flat in Sidcup. She saw that they were fed and clothed and went off to school with enough to eat, but the worry and exertion took its toll and just after their fourteenth birthdays, Hugo and Julian became orphans.

A distant relative of their father, 'Uncle Percy' as he liked to be called, let the boys stay with him and his wife in Northampton, an arrangement that caused friction in an already unhappy relationship, and as soon as Julian was sixteen, he left school and got a job as a trainee in a small factory that produced chemical fertilisers.

Julian's relationship with Hugo had been one of a protective 'younger brother'. Joyce had been able to cope with a teenager with a mental age of five well enough and Julian did his best after she was gone, but with his sights already set on a career in scientific study it became increasingly difficult for him to manage, and he got no help from 'Uncle Percy' and his wife.

Julian had excelled at school, especially in mathematics and science, had found the discipline of laboratory work invigorating and his lively, inquiring mind was stimulated endlessly. One of the few novels he read was 'Arrowsmith' by Sinclair Lewis. It had been given as a prize for outstanding natural science study at school. Julian read it avidly and one of the main protagonists, Doctor Max Gottlieb, assumed the role of hero to the impressionable boy. His maxim that "whenever you think you have solved a problem, doubt it and start again," which he impressed on the young Arrowsmith, became a fundamental for Julian, one which he carried with him into his studies at university. He had kept in touch with his science teacher, Brian Hood, a tall, stooping man who, astonished by Julian's precocity, had arranged a scholarship to Cambridge, his old place of study. It took about a year for the funds to come through but once they did, Julian handed in his notice at the chemical works and headed for Cambridge.

He wrote to Hugo regularly about his time at university but only received occasional replies from 'Uncle Percy' letting him know that Hugo was in good health and in fine spirits. In fact, Hugo had been placed in a council home for the mentally enfeebled. Julian found out when he returned to Northampton on his first Christmas break. He was devastated by the conditions into which his brother had been incarcerated. The placement was legal, there was little Julian could do, except vow to make enough money to rescue Hugo and place him in better surroundings.

Living in the vicinity of death had steeled Julian against life. Instead of taking part in the more traditional activities of his fellow students he began to shun their company, to turn his back on bacchanalia, to get his head down and study, to master the disciplines of his chosen subject, even to dominate them.

Genetics, a science clouded by political and ethical issues, became his subject. He worked feverishly in the laboratory convincing himself that he would, one day, make the breakthrough that would make the difference, not only to the world but for his own status and existence. He followed Max Gottlieb's dictum faithfully—rejecting his findings and starting again—until, frustrated at the slow progress he was making, he decided to abandon any 'rules' and, with the help of Joan, his loyal assistant, he forged into unknown territory. He knew of the advances established molecular biologists were making but he laboured on despite the advice of his tutors to '…try another field, Hawkes' and '…are you sure you're entirely suited to this kind of work?'

His fellow students treated him with a mixture of envy and disdain, knowing that he was putting in the effort that they should have been making. Invitations to the student bar or the pub soon dried up. He became a pariah. Julian soon learned that his isolation was a strength. He worked on feverishly, committed to a goal that he was sure would catapult him beyond the reach of his fellows.

Despite the advances made by established scientists Julian ploughed on. He was close to producing his findings on the accumulation of copper in certain human organs, a condition known as 'Wilson's Disease', when the European Journal of Human Genetics published their own article on the same subject. Julian was devastated. He took the sojourn in Gottingen where his interest in eugenics was born.

A taboo subject in Germany since 1945, he found that there were some who secretly continued to study the science of human engineering. Among them was Professor Josef Meinengen. A tall, willowy man, he didn't advocate the methods or practices of the Nazi era, but he did hold a belief that if mankind was going to survive it had to be judicious in its approach to 'anthropomorphic determining'. Julian learnt of the way the mentally ill had been dealt with by the Nazis and he thought of Hugo, rotting away in a home in England. Questions about the ethics and morals of what he was studying whirled around in his mind and he deluded himself into believing that he could, somehow, help his twin brother.

Julian returned from Germany with aspirations of a different kind from those that had driven him before. Armed with a diploma and a letter of recommendation from Gottingen he gained a junior position on the teaching faculty at Cambridge and began his offensive on Academia. At his interview with a committee of mistrustful-looking Dons, when asked if he had any relatives, he blurted out, 'No, my parents are both dead. I'm an only child.' Afterwards, surprised that he felt no guilt in denying Hugo, he reasoned that he was better off unencumbered by past associations. And when he received the position as Junior Biology Professor his choice seemed justified. From that moment on he was Professor Julian Hawkes, alone against the world.

To that end he cultivated a charisma and charm that captivated not only his students but gradually his peers as well. His good-looks, conviviality and silver-tongue drew large audiences for his, often humorous, always challenging, lectures. The car accident which led to his wife's infirmity helped his cause no end. People who had never even met Joan felt sorry for him and he welcomed their consoling words. With success came financial rewards and he was able to take his brother out of local authority care and place him in a home in Scotland where he was given the care and attention he deserved. Under the name of Hugo Brown, their mother's maiden name, he lived out the rest of his life in quiet seclusion.

As Julian's reputation grew so did his power and soon agencies outside the University were seeking out his thoughts and opinions on topics as diverse as 'teaching sex education to primary school children' and 'the therapeutic benefits of lava lamps'. He was a public relations dream. Newspaper articles, magazine features, television, all courted Professor Julian Hawkes, and it wasn't long before the politicians came calling. A seat on the Scientific Advisory Board gave him access to the workings of government and an insight into power and corruption at the very highest level. He was delighted. It consolidated his growing belief that disorder, and chaos were at the heart of all human activity.

Julian also returned from Germany with a fundamental knowledge of the arcane sciences of alchemy, astrology, and other obscure disciplines. So pleased with his disciple was Professor Meinengen that he had given him an ancient leather-bound tome, the Hermeticum Praxis, that contained the secrets of the Ancients; spells, archaic formula and other esoteric information on the dark arts. He still had the treasured item, which he kept safely locked up in his study. More and more he found its teachings relevant to his research.

Taking on the establishment, shaking the rigid foundations of convention, became a cause for Julian, but underlying all his controversial pronouncements and public relations exercises was the desire for revenge on academia and the establishment. It became his secret obsession. He didn't question the motivation for this intense craving—whether it was guilt at the abandonment of his brother or the lack of a recognisable father-figure Julian had no time for pseudo-psychoanalytical explanations. He considered gazing backward hampered looking forward. He had his mind set and he had set it. The task of creating a new Julian Hawkes had commenced. Social engineering worked. He was living proof. The next step was the adventurous one.

Reaching beyond the cosy confines of conventional science into a dangerous, disordered world.

Now, with all ties to the University and other civil agencies severed he was ready to set off on the Great Adventure.

Chapter 5

Sitting in the darkest corner of the back bar in the Golden Unicorn on Bridge Street sat a thin, pale-looking, young man. Thomas Alfred Creighton drained another pint of beer. There were five empty glasses already on the table. Dark rings around the eyes that contained pinprick sized pupils betrayed his aberrant lifestyle. Every now and then he glanced up at the other customers in the bar as if he was waiting for someone and when a well-dressed Asian man appeared at the bar and ordered a glass of wine, Thomas Alfred Creighton took note, and a febrile look of anticipation crossed his gaunt features. The Asian man, clearly a regular, joked with the barman and a few of the customers then left his drink on the bar and headed towards the toilets. As he passed by Creighton he stumbled, bumped into the table, apologised, and moved on. But the delivery had been successful - a small envelope imperceptibly handed over from dealer to client. Creighton stood up and left the pub quickly. As he did so another customer, standing on the far side of the back room, watched him go, finished his beer, and followed.

Outside it was cold and murky. A damp night on the streets of Cambridge. Creighton hurried away into the blackness of the side streets evading the main roads with their hazy lamps. His pursuer kept a discreet distance, but he was on safe ground. Creighton only had one thing on his mind - an instant fix - he was oblivious to everything else. After a few minutes Creighton let himself into a small, shabby terraced house in a rather run-down part of town.

The living room resembled the mind of its sole occupier. Beer cans, empty pizza boxes, dirty plates, cigarette stubs, books, newspapers, and clothes were strewn about. The television had been left on. Creighton dashed in, crouched down, swept some of the debris from the coffee table and started to unfold the envelope and was about to cut a line of the white powder when he heard a sound. A thought passed through his mind, 'did I leave the front door open?' He hesitated, the razor blade in his shaking hand hovered over the 'release from torment' before him. Another sound, the door closing and a footstep. A figure appeared in the shadows by the curtained windows.

Unnerved, Creighton got to his feet. 'Who are you? What d'you want?' Despite his unkempt appearance Creighton spoke with a rather posh, although groggy, voice. The figure took a step forward.

'Thomas Alfred Creighton. One-time medical student, with all the promise of becoming, perhaps, a leading surgeon or consultant. But instead became a student drop-out'.

Julian stepped into the light. He had one hand in his coat pocket which contained a loaded revolver. He had purchased it on the black market through a friend of a friend. You never could tell with 'druggies' and 'piss artists' he had convinced himself. He leant forward and turned off the television.

'Hey leave that… I was watching it…' Creighton dropped the razor blade. 'Are you the police?'

Julian continued. 'Drunk, drug addict, petty criminal, shoplifter, burglar, on benefits. Future rather bleak.'

'So what?' bleated the terrified young man. 'And I'm not an addict. The weed is just for fun.'

Julian sneered. 'Then you won't have any trouble giving it

up, will you?'

'If you're not the police, who are you, and what's it got to do with you what I am?'

Julian moved closer. 'Twenty-five now. Dead by twenty-nine if not sooner. Mourned by none.' He added, as an inducement, 'unless...'

Creighton was confused but realised that this was no 'official' call. This was no Social Worker or Drug Help-Line Visitor, and it certainly wasn't the police who had knocked him around and turned the place upside-down on their last visit. 'Unless what?' he managed to say.

'What was it that sent you on that downward path, Thomas Alfred Creighton?' asked Julian.

'None of your business.'

'But it is my business. You are my business. I am in a position to make you an offer.'

'Another bloody do-gooder! I might have known.'

Julian came closer. 'My offer has nothing to do with doing good.'

Creighton was taken aback momentarily and then he recognised Julian. 'You're that chap on the telly, that Professor. The controversial one.'

Ignoring him, Julian went on. 'In fact, my offer has positively sinister implications.'

Creighton was by now confused but also slightly intrigued. From the back of his alcohol and cocaine befuddled mind came recollections of a time spent in the lecture halls of medical school, of competent endeavour and academic success.

Julian recognised that his quarry was weakening. 'It's a chance, Thomas Alfred Creighton, to get even. To pay back for the years of insult and injury.'

Creighton grimaced as he remembered and as he collapsed onto the leather sofa. 'I was a grammar schoolboy. They gave it to me good and proper,' he bitterly let out by way of explanation. And then he instantly regretted his outburst, recognising that he may have given something away.

So forceful was Julian's presence that Creighton had forgotten all about his 'fix'. Julian regarded him with studied impassivity. The younger man's demeanour was no longer desperate and feverish but had become   calm and melancholic. His features, long unkempt hair, and stubble notwithstanding, were not unpleasant. Round brown eyes and an aquiline nose gave him an almost aristocratic air. His clothes looked as if he had not taken them off for a week.

Julian reached into his jacket pocket, took out his wallet and produced a business card which he placed on the table next to the envelope. 'Die a slow lingering death or begin again. The choice is up to you,' said Julian.

'Why should I?' Creighton replied, but with little conviction.

Realising that he would have to offer more than just words Julian took a wad of ten-pound notes from his wallet and threw them down. 'This is just to help you get started, a haircut, clean clothes. A bath will cost you nothing. More could follow'. He watched as Creighton became agitated; he was clearly tempted by the money.   Julian then withdrew, leaving the young man to struggle with his demons.

On the drive back to the 'Mendes House' Julian considered the possible consequences of his actions. He thought it unlikely that Creighton would go 'cold turkey' and give up his drug habit but was convinced that the   money, and the promise of more, would sway him. In the end, he surmised, Creighton would either get his 'fix', return to the pub, and get drunk, or he would take the bait. There was no point in worrying. In any event he was relieved that he hadn't needed the revolver which he had transferred from his coat pocket to the glove compartment. He pressed down on the accelerator and sped down the dark country lane.

Julian had begun his new job at the Davos Corporation a few days before. It had been in the contract that he could have an assistant, but someone of his choosing. Joan would have been perfect; loyal, obedient, discreet, and good at her work. However, she would have baulked at the kind of work he was proposing to do. She was too decent, she had moral scruples. It was her one failing.

On his first day Julian was visited in his brand-new laboratory by Doctor Speelman, the Director of the works. A large, round kindly man in his sixties, Speelman had been the business manager at Sanguis Pharmaceuticals in Switzerland. After a scandal involving contaminated blood, the company closed down, but Speelman was head-hunted by Davos in California to run their European base. He was a canny businessman who knew enough about the research side of medicine to justify his position.

'Professor Hawkes. Welcome.' They shook hands. 'The Davos Foundation is at your service.' Julian regarded all in 'management' with a degree of suspicion. He liked Speelman but was wary of him. Research was tolerated as long as it led to profits.

He asked about Julian's laboratory assistant.

'I have someone in mind. A promising student.'

'From Cambridge?'

'Is that important?'

'Not necessarily, I just assumed.'

Julian cast an inquiring look around the room.

'The centrifuge?'

'It's here. Installation will be underway later today.'

'And the animals, Doctor Speelman?' Julian examined the empty cages dotted around the laboratory.

'On their way. As requested. They should start to arrive today. And the chemicals you ordered. Some of them rather odd, I have to say. And the plants in the conservatory.'

'Odd?'

'Fucitol? I've never come across it before.'

'It's a sugar alcohol. Comes from seaweed,' Julian replied in a dismissive manner. That seemed to end the meeting, at least as far as Julian was concerned. Speelman, a little deflated, convinced himself that his new Head of Research was temperamental and perhaps a little nervous too, and so he turned to leave. 'Perhaps we could lunch together...'

'Certainly,' said Julian who was opening and closing cupboards and drawers checking on the equipment at his disposal. At the doorway Speelman hesitated, then said. 'Oh, Professor... about the key to this door...'

'Yes. I have it,' said Julian. 'The other is with security at the gatehouse.'

Speelman was clearly uneasy about this arrangement and Julian sensed his disquiet. 'It's in the contract that I alone have access to the lab. Unless there's a fire, of course.' Speelman smiled weakly and backed out, leaving Julian alone in his new place of work.

The next day, Alfred Thomas Creighton presented himself to the security guard at the gatehouse and after a number of phone-calls he was admitted to the laboratory. At first Julian didn't recognise him. His hair was short, he had bathed and shaved, his clothes were modest and respectable and, Julian noted, there was some colour in his cheeks, a sign that he may have had a proper breakfast.

Creighton had stared at the business card and the money for a full ten minutes before picking up the card, reading the name on it, then counting out the notes—four hundred and fifty pounds. Baffled, he sat in the semi-darkness trying to work out what had just happened. What was it the man had said? '... dead at twenty-nine... mourned by no one...' that was certainly true, he had no living relatives. And what about '... sinister implications...?' What could he have meant by that? Creighton got up and paced back and forth across the untidy room. It had never crossed his mind to want to get even with anybody. If he'd thought at all about his scholarly demise, he would have put it down to falling in with the wrong crowd or a lack of staying power or just plain bad luck. But from somewhere in the back of his addled mind the idea of revenge began to emerge and took on intriguing possibilities. There was that fellow student who had 'stolen' his girlfriend. He was an oarsman, an American, Brad something, who just flexed his muscles and off she went. He didn't blame her... what was her name? He stopped pacing, sat down, and took stock.

And, yes, he thought he had recognised his strange caller. He searched for the remote controller and turned on the television, called up the Teletext news channel and scrolled through the items until he came to, *'Controversial Professor Julian Hawkes resigns from Senior Post...'* His mind was racing by now. He rummaged amongst the items swept from the table and found a day-old tabloid. Turning the pages rapidly he came across the article, headlined, *'Senior Government Advisor quits...'* and there was a photograph taken outside Downing Street a few years ago, of his night visitor together with that chubby chap with wild hair who had become Prime Minister. A vague recollection surfaced, of falling asleep during one of the esteemed Professor's lectures. It was during Creighton's second year and by then he was drinking heavily and puffing on the occasional spliff. What was going on? What did the notorious Professor want with me? mused Creighton.

By the time the first glimmers of light came through the curtains Creighton had made up his mind. In an act of extreme desperation, sweat breaking out on his body, hands shaking, he tried to flush the white powder down the toilet. *No,* he thought, *I'll keep it...* just in case. And he folded up the envelope and placed it in a kitchen drawer. Perhaps I'll sell it on, make a bit on the side. Immediately he regretted what he had done but after a few cups of black coffee and a long walk in the early morning chill he partially recovered and, oddly, felt a certain sense of release.

Later that day, he recalled the words of Professor Hawkins, 'Then you won't have any trouble giving it up, will you?' And he realised it hadn't been much of a struggle and a new confidence began to grow within him.

Emboldened by the experience he had used some of the money to pay off a few debts, dusted off the suit that he'd bought for his graduation, had it dry-cleaned and then visited the barber's shop. And that evening he took a long, luxurious bath.

After Julian had spent the day showing his new assistant the laboratory, the large greenhouse, and the other facilities—he was especially drawn to the rats and monkeys—just as they were about to leave, Julian took Creighton's arm in a firm grip. 'What did you do with the drugs?'

'What?'

'The other night…'

'I flushed them down the toilet,' replied Creighton.

'You're not a very convincing liar.'

He didn't know what to say. He shook himself free from Julian's grasp. 'I didn't take any if that's what you mean?'

Julian knew that Creighton had been impressed with the facility, that his interest in things scientific had been rekindled. At one point, as they walked through the hot house he had asked, 'what kind of work will we be doing, sir?' Julian liked the 'sir', it conferred on him instant nobility, and said that they would discuss their work later.

Now the time had come. 'All right, Thomas Alfred Creighton, this is the plan. We start tomorrow with the research work. Nothing that any other research laboratory isn't doing. Once the management here are happy with our slow and gentle progress and once you are happy with my working methods, then the real work begins.'

Creighton was curious. 'Real work?'

Julian noticed no 'sir' this time. He took an envelope from the pocket of his lab coat. 'If you fail me, in any way, you'll wish you'd never been born.' He handed over the envelope and watched as Creighton peered inside. He was embarrassed but also gratified with the contents. 'I told you. I'm off the weed.'

'There's a little extra, on top of your first week's salary, as well,' said Julian. Creighton stuffed the envelope in his pocket and left the laboratory. Julian hung up his lab coat, put on his jacket, turned out the lights and locked the door behind him.

'What's he like?'

'Who?'

'Your new assistant, my surrogate.'

He had mentioned Creighton to Joan, and she was keen to know if he was up to the mark.

'I think he'll work out fine. Of course, he could never replace you.'

'Very diplomatic of you, husband.' Joan had been happy for him, glad that he was in a more independent environment but still there was the inner restlessness. She had convinced herself that it was his nature. As his assistant she had been able to bear some of his unease but now, helpless, a cripple, bed-bound, there was little she could do except try to understand. 'It is what you want, Julian, isn't it?'

'Of course,' he replied confidently. 'And with the extra money I'll be earning we'll see about that operation in Switzerland.'

She said nothing. Her expression changed to one of resignation.

'It's what we've talked about, what you've wanted ever since…' He broke off, suddenly recalling their vow not to mention certain past events.

'It could mean…'

'Yes, could,' she interrupted him bitterly.

He was worried about her reluctance to see a Consultant Surgeon, a specialist in spinal injuries, who had been recommended to him and his anxiety turned to anger. 'If you won't help yourself.'

'I'm sorry, Julian,' she began to sob.

'It's no good crying over spilt milk,' and he left her and went down to his laboratory. Looking around the room it seemed small and ill-equipped compared to the new facility at Davos.

The following weeks he was hardly at home. Joan heard him

drive away before six every morning and he didn't return until late at night. Sometimes in the early hours she would be woken by the sound of his car pulling up on the gravel drive, the car door slamming, the key in the front door and his weary-sounding footsteps up the stairs and the closing of the door to his room. She blamed herself at first and then began to wonder if all his time was being spent at work. There had been other women, of that she was sure. He was a man, after all, and his public profile was such that others must have been attracted in the same way that, all those years ago, she had been attracted. But whatever happened between them and there had been heated exchanges before, she knew that, before long, her bedroom door would open and he would enter, a broad smile on his face, sit on the bed and they would play a hand of whist and talk about the day's events as if nothing had come between them.

Creighton, wearing a white lab coat, obviously sober and considerably healthier, but still with dark rings around his eyes, was feeding an albino rat in a plastic cage. A group of wealthy patrons and public figures were being shown around the laboratory by Doctor Speelman and Julian. Amongst the group was the Junior Minister for Education, Maurice Bond. Julian hadn't laid eyes on him since that notorious lecture. Now, somewhat alarmed by how young he appeared, he wondered what he was doing here. 'Always interested in 'things Scientific', he explained in a quiet moment, and he pressed his business card into Julian's hand.

'When you have a moment…' came the invitation, much to Julian's surprise.

Julian turned away. 'So far our experiments have showed a fifty per cent increase in the production of antibodies…

Creighton!'

Creighton jerked to attention, opened the cage, and took out a large white rat. The visitors feigned interest.

'These are the only animals used in experiments by the foundation. As you can see, they are perfectly healthy and well cared for.'

'Funny looking critter,' an elderly American commented.

'Albinos. Bred here on the premises. Thank you, Creighton...'

Doctor Speelman appeared pleased and smiled at Julian as the entourage moved on. As they passed, Creighton delivered a subservient bow. Doctor Speelman seemed unnerved by this odd gesture.

They had been working on the gene replacement experiment for some weeks. Quite a few specimens had died, and it had taken careful dosages to get the right balance. Creighton was enjoying the tasks set by Professor Hawkins but wondered when the 'real work' was to start. His drug and alcohol intake had decreased by some measure since taking the job. On occasion, he still succumbed to temptation but was careful to hide any outward signs of abuse. Julian, of course, knew what was going on and, one morning, when Creighton was late for work and Doctor Speelman had questioned the Professor's choice of assistant, Julian had turned on him and pointed out that for the miserable wage on offer they were lucky to get anyone. And, he added, Creighton was a hard worker and did as he was told. The following day Creighton got a raise in salary, and the issue was never brought up again.

Speelman returned that afternoon after lunching with the patrons and assured Julian that they had been bowled over with the progress he had made not to mention with the humane treatment of the animals.

'They might have been not so impressed had they been shown this.' Julian lifted a gauze that covered a plastic cage containing a variety of rats. One of the rats, larger, an albino specimen, corralled and cornered the others. Speelman lent forward and studied their behaviour.

'Surely, the dominant male?'

Julian nodded to Creighton who dropped a morsel of cheese into the opposite corner of the cage. When one of the smaller brown rats attempted to escape, the albino rat launched a vicious attack before turning to eat the cheese. The other rats stayed cowering in the corner.

Speelman's eyes widened as he studied the scene before him. Julian handed over a sheaf of papers. 'Read the reports, judge for yourself.' The older man glanced at the papers, but his attention soon returned to the animals in the cage. The brown rats were now acting submissively to the albino.

'A genetically superior specimen. A 'Super Rat' if you like.'

'I never thought it possible.'

'When you hire the best, Doctor Speelman, you get the best,' Julian arrogantly replied.

Speelman, a naturally cautious man, was suddenly fearful. His brow broke out in a sweat, his expression changed to one of extreme concern. 'This must be kept amongst ourselves… for now. When the time is right, I'll present your findings to our parent body in California…'

Julian maintained a defiant stance. 'As you wish, Doctor. Meanwhile, I shall carry on with my research.'

'Of course, of course… just be discreet.'

Julian laughed to himself as Speelman hurried out of the laboratory. 'Well done, Creighton.'

As Creighton was covering over the rat's cage Julian continued, 'Your work has been exemplary. Now that our employers are, or will be, otherwise engaged, we shall commence something a little more daring.'

'You mean…?'

'We will convene at your home later this evening. I trust you will make the place a little more conducive to entertaining than before?'

The next day, intrigued by Maurice Bond's invitation, Julian called him, and a meeting was arranged for the following day in London. On the train down to the capitol he reflected on last night's session with the belligerent Creighton. He knew how difficult it was going to be to persuade someone to commit murder and he had used every possible argument, eventually resorting to blackmail and physical intimidation. The blackmail came in the form of a large amount of money and the promise of more, in addition there was a considerable amount of cocaine. And after grabbing him by his collar and roughing up the young man, Creighton was won over. As Julian laid out the plan, he noticed that Creighton became rather enthusiastic. Julian detected a certain calculation in Creighton's acquiescence and later, on the train, realised how dangerous his 'assistant' could be. He would have to tread very carefully.

The rendezvous took place in a small bistro behind the Palace of Westminster. Julian was, once again, struck by how youthful Maurice Bond looked and he couldn't help remarking on the fact.

'Monkey glands,' came the reply and he laughed. 'You're not the first to comment.' His casual manner and general bonhomie was infectious. After a few pleasantries and a mention of their last sighting of each other, 'fairly disastrous, I'd say,' recalled the Junior Minister. 'Did you really believe all that stuff?

'Absolutely,' replied Julian.

Again, Maurice laughed. 'We'd wondered what happened to you after all the resignations.'

'I had no choice,' Julian said haughtily.

'No, no… of course not.'

There was a pause in which both studied each other. Julian wondered what was coming next.

'Actually, it was no accident that I turned up at Davos the other day.'

Julian was not surprised.

'Your work there. Rats and monkeys. Interesting, is it?' Julian didn't respond.

'I mean, your lecture indicated an interest in, shall we say, other branches of research.'

Again, Julian maintained a non-reply reply.

'Let me be more specific, Professor Hawkes…'

'I wish you would, Mister Bond,' interrupted Julian.

'The new government has a remit to come up with new ways of reforming certain aspects of public institutional life.'

Maurice Bond lowered his voice. 'Certain, shall we say, interested parties are talking with government about ways to relieve pressure on the public purse. I must stress that we are only talking… at present.'

'Are you here as the Junior Minister for Education, or?' asked Julian cannily.

Maurice laughed and then assumed a more serious expression. 'I represent a group of people, highly placed people, who are like-minded and view the present situation with some foreboding.'

'What's that got to do with me?'

'If I'm not mistaken, and judging by your fractious relationship with academia, I would consider you, 'like-minded.'

Julian was puzzled and, of course, flattered. But why doesn't he get to the point, he wondered.

Maurice continued, somewhat haltingly, as if he was under orders to not give too much away. 'I am, first and foremost, an elected official… and therefore responsible to my constituents… but… times change… new ways   of doing things have to be considered… and there are certain scientific disciplines… frowned upon nowadays…   that could prove useful in the future…'

'Such as?' shot back Julian. He noticed that the affable Junior Minister was beginning to sweat a little.

'Well… as I said, we are just talking at the moment, but… I trust that when our talks become more concrete, I   can call on you?'

Julian settled back. 'Typical politico,' he mused, 'always beating around the bush'. But he knew exactly what was on the agenda. He laughed inwardly, then said, 'Of course you may call on me.'

They parted on good terms and agreed to meet again at a later date. Just as they left the bistro, Julian had   asked, in his customary blunt manner, if there was any money on the table if future 'talks' proved fruitful. 'More than you can imagine,' came the reply. As he returned to Cambridge on the evening train, he pondered on the power of blackmail to influence human affairs.

Chapter 6

One evening, a few days later, in a pub close to Corpus Christi College, a handsome, tall, athletic young man, Archie Brasher, was entertaining a group of fellow undergraduates and locals at the bar. He was used to being the focus of attention, whether in the classroom or on the sports field. Piercing blue eyes, a shock of blonde hair and an eloquent speaking voice held his audience in thrall.

'…so, there I was, and don't forget I'm over there on a sports scholarship, in this Tokyo nightclub as a guest of the coach of the Olympic swimming team when a couple come out on to the stage, strip off and get ready to perform…'

A couple of the young people gasped, others sniggered, and more drinks were ordered.

'…when all of a sudden the chap in charge halts proceedings and yours truly is invited up on stage.' More gasps and laughter from some.

'I don't believe a word,' expressed a small student standing nearby.

'You're making it up, Brasher.' He was ignored.

'The bloke steps aside and the girl spreads herself ready for me.'

'Blimey! What did you do, Archie?'

'It's a custom over there apparently. Kowtowing to the Westerner and all that.'

'Yes, but what did you do?

'What do you think I did... in front of a hundred or so Japanese businessmen?'

'Did you rise to the occasion?' asked one of the locals.

Laughter all around.

'Did you fuck her?'

Brasher grinned, took a long draught of his ale and said, 'Mind your own bloody business.'

More laughter drowned out the few disappointed sneers and the group broke up. His girlfriend of the moment, Louise, a mousey red head, hung on his arm and gazed at him admiringly. 'You never told me that story, Archie.'

'You never asked.' He was disdainful towards the women who spun in and out of his orbit, generally preferring the company of fellow sporty types. Archie was in his last year at Cambridge. It was acknowledged that he would graduate with full honours, both for his academic work and for his sporting prowess.

He ordered another pint, his fifth, from the barman and a glass of wine for Louise. He was proud of the amount of alcohol he could down without any aftereffects. 'I need to take a 'Fraser'...' he barked out and headed off towards the toilet. A few moments later, having relieved himself and splashed some cold water on his face, he reappeared and was about to join his friends at the bar when he noticed, sitting alone at a corner table, a vaguely familiar figure. He stepped closer.

'Creighton? It is you, isn't it. You didn't used to wear glasses?'

'Brasher...' Creighton feigned surprise.

'What the hell happened to you? I mean, you just disappeared.'

Creighton finished off his half pint of Guinness and gestured

53

towards the bar. 'Funny story. Any of it true?' Archie sat down opposite him. 'You were really bright.'

'Thank you. Not so good at sports though.'

'There was a rumour going around that you'd hit the skids and were doing all sorts of bad stuff?'

Creighton managed a smile. 'You first,' he said.

They had met in their first year and, although not close friends, had been aware of each other's achievements. When Creighton failed to appear for the second term, Archie was surprised but, as he reflected at the time, there were quite a few who dropped out.

'Another?' Archie asked.

'Thanks.'

Archie returned a few moments later with a glass of Guinness and his own pint of ale. 'Tell me... Tom, what have you been up to?' He gestured at Creighton's attire. 'You look as though you're doing all right.'

Creighton had been sent out by Julian to buy a brand-new set of clothes. 'Make yourself look the part of a successful, respectable man of business,' he had said, and Creighton duly set out to buy a couple of new suits, shirts, ties, and two pairs of brogue shoes. Julian had also urged him to wear a pair of thick-framed glasses, 'They'll give you gravitas'.

'I'm doing... well, thank you, Archie,' he replied. 'And what about you?' They talked on for some time. Archie was more than interested in what his old acquaintance had to say, but mostly he talked about himself, as Julian had said he would. His girlfriend had at one point tried to inveigle herself into their conversation, but Archie had been rude to her, and she walked out of the pub, tears in her eyes. They began to discuss girls.

Archie, as was his wont, bragged about the number he had

seduced. Creighton was more discreet. Julian had advised him that if he was to succeed in his task he would have to 'box clever' with his prey.

As Archie downed yet another pint and insisted that he buy another round, Creighton recalled the evening at his house where Julian had laid bare his intentions.

Julian read from a prepared dossier. 'Archibald Brasher-Courtney. Known amongst his fellow students as 'Brasher'. Scion of a family that can trace its ancestry back to the Plantagenets. Parents separated. Father, a successful economist who has worked for the World Bank. Mother, a musician and artist, runs an art gallery in New York. Measles, mumps, chicken pox as a child. No other serious medical defects or conditions. Twenty-twenty vision. Academically brilliant. Set to get a First in Applied Mathematics. Speaks four languages fluently. A Cambridge Blue, played in two Varsity matches. Captain of the University cricket team. A dozen first class centuries already to his name. Olympic swimming hopeful, having achieved several qualifying times. A bright, successful future ahead of him. I shall regret the sacrifice he is about to make...'

Julian went on to explain how he had chosen his quarry carefully and that he, Creighton, was to play an integral part in the scheme and how to use the lure of sex in the entrapment. Creighton shivered in anticipation, sensing that something terrible was going to happen. As ever, Julian had finished his talk with the warning, '... and if you fail me your life will not be worth living.'

The pub was emptying of customers. 'These young girls,' Archie said dismissively, gesturing towards the female students some of whom were still at the bar, '... don't you find them rather... juvenile? Wouldn't you prefer a more mature class of woman?' Archie had boasted that of course he had visited certain establishments in Soho, but Creighton knew he was bragging. He invited Archie back to his house to, 'meet a certain lady he knew who provided a special service.' Archie, impressed with Creighton's prosperous appearance and his savoir-faire manner, accepted. In truth he had become a little weary of student life and was already looking forward to graduation and getting out into the real world. And here was his 'old chum' as he was calling Creighton by now, who had done just that.

Twenty minutes later, Archie was lounging on the sofa in Creighton's living room. He was quite drunk and kept nagging his host to get in touch with this 'certain lady' and to get him another drink. Archie had moved on to spirits and as Creighton pretended to make the call he mixed a powerful sleeping draught, provided by Julian, into Archie's glass of vodka. A few minutes later Creighton watched as the victim swallowed his medicine and slipped off into the arms of Morpheus.

In his upstairs bedroom Creighton took off his glasses and quickly changed into some more suitable clothes and was pulling on a polo-necked jumper when he heard the low throb of Julian's sports car approaching. He looked out of the window and saw the car come to a stop in the alley behind the house. He dashed downstairs, managed, with some difficulty, to hoist Archie's body over his shoulder in a fireman's carry and stumbled through the kitchen and out into the yard. It was dark and a veil of mist hung over the silent town. Julian opened the boot of the car and Creighton dumped the body inside.

The journey took nearly an hour. Julian was careful not to go too fast. 'You gave him the whole amount?'

Creighton nodded. 'It was easy,' he added, somewhat

surprised.

'You didn't leave any traces of 'our friend' at your house?' Julian was being ultra-cautious. Creighton was irked by his lack of trust in his assistant. 'None', he replied tersely.

The security guard at the Davos Foundation was used to Julian turning up at odd hours and waved him through the barrier. The car park was empty, but Julian parked as near to the rear entrance of the conservatory, where he knew there were no security cameras, as he could. They carried Archie's still limp body into the glasshouse and deposited it on the stone floor next to a specially prepared patch of bare soil. Their efforts were lighted by a watery half-moon which shone down through the glass roof.

Julian looked down triumphantly at the prone figure, 'Let's get to work then.' He then produced the leather-bound tome, the Hermeticum Praxis, that Professor Meinengen had awarded him.

'What's that?' asked Creighton.

'Our guide into another world,' replied a feverish voice. Julian opened it at the relevant page and studied the drawings and their accompanying text.

'The rope?'

'I've got it.'

Creighton hurried over to a small area within the glasshouse and moments later appeared with a long rope.

'It is hemp? Not Manila hemp or synthetic?' demanded Julian.

'As prescribed. I had to go to a chandler down by the Thames to get it.'

As Julian began to form one end of the rope into a noose Creighton, as instructed, removed the unconscious man's trousers and underpants. At the precise moment the noose was placed around Archie's neck the effects of the sleeping draught began to wear off and he stirred, snorted, and his eyes began to open in narrow slits.

'Quickly,' exhorted Julian. Creighton threw the other end of the rope over one of the metal girders that supported the glass roof. Both began to pull on the rope. As the noose tightened around Archie's neck, and as he was lifted from the ground, he coughed and spluttered. Suddenly, his athletic body began to react to its inelegant posture but the ensuing struggles, arms flailing, legs twisting and turning, were futile as he was hoisted up above the bare patch of earth. Creighton and Julian were soaked with sweat by the time they secured the rope to a stanchion, and they stood watching for what seemed an eternity as Archie's attempts to cling on to a life with so much promise ended, and his lifeless body swung gently in the air.

Creighton noted the contrast between the student's clothed upper body and his naked lower parts and was about to comment when a firm hand gesture from Julian stopped him. Creighton looked over at his master's aquiline profile, highlighted by the pale moon, giving him a look of insane arrogance. He had become another person, thought Creighton, a madman, a devilish creature. The very archetype of the mad professor.

Julian again referred to the Hermeticum Praxis. 'And now...' he uttered in a breathless whisper. They both watched spellbound as a few drops of semen were expressed from Archie's limp penis and landed on the bare earth beneath his feet. Julian's eyes gleamed with triumph as he leaned forward and closely observed the white sperm mingling with the soil. Another drop fell to the earth. Julian stood up straight and turned to his assistant, now his accomplice.

'You think I'm mad, don't you?'

Creighton was, for a moment, speechless, being in awe but also terrified. 'If you are, then so am I,' he replied.

'A good answer, Creighton.' Julian turned back to the patch of impregnated ground and, with a trowel, lightly covered the damp area with dry soil. 'Let's tidy up now...' With some effort they lowered the body down. Archie's face was frozen in a rictus of agony which Creighton found unsettling.

'Never seen a dead man before?'

Creighton shook his head, wound up the rope into a coil and deposited it and the trowel in the car. Then the two conspirators carried the dead youth from the glasshouse, dumped his lifeless, spent body into the boot, and left the scene.

Creighton crawled into bed a few hours later, drained but also strangely exhilarated by the night's events. They had driven out into the countryside bordering a fen, where Archie's body was weighed down with concrete blocks and submerged into a remote ditch. Julian had picked out the spot weeks earlier.

Later that night, Creighton reflected that because everything had been so carefully planned and had gone off without a hitch, he had to admire Professor Julian Hawkes. And, he wondered, what made him turn from a career of ethical endeavour to one of base criminality. As he drifted off into a deep sleep it seemed that life had become more exciting and rewarding for Thomas Alfred Creighton.

A few days later, Julian was in the greenhouse checking the temperature gauge, examining the bare patch of earth, feeling the surface of the soil, adding a few drops of water. He stared down impatiently, as if willing green shoots to appear on his command.

On his return to the laboratory a rather nervous-looking Creighton placed the local newspaper in front of him.

'Mysterious disappearance of promising student baffles police force' read the headline.

'The police were asking questions in the pub, you know, where I picked him up.'

Julian was unmoved, threw the paper into a waste bin.

'They asked his girlfriend if she remembered the man he was last seen talking to.'

'And did she?'

Creighton recovered the newspaper from the bin and read out, 'It says here that she described - *a man of about forty years of age, smartly dressed, with glasses and brogue shoes.'*

'What did you do with the clothes you bought? Did you dispose of them as I instructed?'

Not yet. I thought…

'I'll do the thinking, Creighton. And the glasses?'

'Oh, I threw them in a skip.'

Julian adopted a paternal manner. 'Take a few days off. Go to the coast and distribute the clothes and shoes in various charity shops. Make sure there is nothing in the pockets.' He reached into his jacket pocket and produced a brown envelope which he pressed into the palm of Creighton's hand. 'If you appear at all nervous people will notice.'

Creighton stuffed the envelope into the pocket of his lab coat and walked over to the animal cages. Julian kept a careful eye on his assistant for the rest of the day and as they were leaving that evening, it was a Tuesday, Creighton said, 'I'll be back on Thursday.'

'And make sure you are,' replied Julian. And sure enough, he was.

Julian had known this moment would come. Joan had shown

him the same headline that morning.

'Did you know him? Was he one of your students?' she inquired.

'The name rings a bell.'

'I should think it would. Archibald Brasher-Courtney. Fancy being saddled with that moniker for life.' Julian laughed. 'He'll probably turn up in some brothel in Paris.'

'Is that what students do these days?'

'I think it's what young men have always done,' he replied.

'You didn't.'

He didn't need to state that he was different, she knew that. She was trying to goad him, and he knew it. This was the first time she had seen him for weeks. He had brought her breakfast tray up and she wondered what had motivated him to do it. 'How is your work coming along, husband?'

He glanced at his watch and got up from the bed. 'I must go. I have an important meeting.' And before she could say anything else he was gone.

Over the next few weeks, Creighton was the model employee, taking on jobs responsibly, making himself readily available for any tasks that Julian pushed his way.

A week after Archie had, somewhat unwillingly, enriched the soil in the conservatory the first green shoot appeared. Julian instructed Creighton in the strict timetable of watering, feeding and observation and it was while he was carrying out the former that Doctor Speelman came across him carefully dripping the required amount of water onto the budding plant.

'We have a very expensive watering system installed. Does this plant require special attention?'

'Professor Hawkins precise instructions, sir,' replied

Creighton.

'Oh... What is it?'

'Mandragora, sir.'

Doctor Speelman was none the wiser.

'A sub-tropical plant from the Mediterranean region. Used in native medicines.'

Speelman had never liked Julian's choice of assistant. He found him supercilious and secretive but was too much in awe of his Head of Research to say anything. Speelman mumbled a response and moved on.

Creighton watched him go then carried on with his task. He fed the shoot with a few drops of specially prepared liquid fertilizer, spread a teaspoonful of blood and bone around the tiny stem, checked the temperature in the greenhouse and wrote down the results in a logbook that Julian had insisted be kept up to date. Creighton was happy to comply and spent a large part of his day in the glasshouse caring for the Mandragora. He often wondered what was going to be the outcome of this special treatment— Julian had told him nothing of the next stage of the experiment. However, as he speculated and as he tended the burgeoning plant, he was perhaps unaware that his part in its creation was causing him to adopt a very protective attitude towards it. Over the next few weeks, as the Mandragora grew, Julian, with some concern, had noticed that Creighton's attention was becoming over-protective. In fact, to his dismay, he noticed that his assistant was assuming an obsessive relationship with the plant.

'Thank goodness,' he reflected, 'the time is near when the experiment will be over, and I can dispense with the services of Thomas Alfred Creighton.'

Chapter 7

'Creighton. I asked you to find me a dog.' Julian, clearly impatient, was wearing his white lab coat, his hands thrust into the pockets. The conservatory was dark, the only light coming from a recently installed security lamp on the outside wall.

The Mandragora was now fully grown. Large oval soft green leaves with a crown of violet flowers in the centre, it stood about four feet tall. Both Julian and his assistant gazed at it with a sense of pride and achievement.

'It's in my car.' Creighton dashed out of the hot house. It was just after midnight, a cool autumnal evening. A small white van that had 'Davos' written discreetly on the side stood outside. Julian had sanctioned the use of the vehicle for laboratory use only and Creighton was named the designated driver. After a quick nervous glance around he opened the back of the van, pulled out a scruffy-looking mongrel on a leash and dragged it into the greenhouse.

Julian was once again referring to his Hermeticum Praxis. A shallow trench was being excavated around the plant exposing the top of the root system. 'Where did you find it?' he asked staring down at the unassuming animal.

'I heard some kids calling out 'Monty, Monty,' in the park. I got to him first.' Julian immediately became irate but before he could speak Creighton, by now used to his master's irrational outbursts, continued.

'Don't worry. No one saw me.'

Julian grabbed the leash. 'Now you will see where science meets sorcery!' He dragged the terrified dog onto the patch of earth and tied the leash firmly around the base of the plant. 'Monty' tugged and scrabbled against the soil in an effort to escape. Julian took a dog biscuit from his pocket and held it out. The dog was momentarily distracted, then strained even more. Julian stepped back, still proffering the lure. The plant, its roots desperately clinging to the earth, began to loosen its grip. 'Put your hands over your ears, Creighton,' he yelled at his mystified but intrigued assistant. Julian continued to tempt the dog. 'Here Monty…' and just as the Mandragora was torn from the ground he dropped the biscuit and clapped his hands over his ears.

The hot house was filled with a terrible, high-pitched, scream. Creighton recalled afterwards that the sound was not unlike that of a hysterical human voice. When silence once again returned to the hot house, 'Monty' lay dead on the floor.

'Look around outside. Make sure no one else heard the noise,' Julian commanded. Creighton obeyed and a few moments later returned and shook his head.

Julian rushed forward and seized the uprooted plant. He examined the foliage and the root system carefully. Creighton was not only puzzled by the spectacle but also extremely unsettled. Julian held up the plant, examined the bifurcated tuber and compared it with a diagram in the ancient tome. Then he spoke in a strange, sinister voice that Creighton had never heard before. 'Go and catch a falling star, Get with child a mandrake root, Tell me where all past years are, Or who cleft the devil's foot…'

Creighton peered at the twisted root. In the gloom it gradually seemed to take on the shape of the human form, a torso, legs, spindly arms, and a twist of hair. Terrified, he stepped back into the shadows.

'Get rid of the dog, take it back to where you found it and make sure you're not seen,' ordered Julian. 'I'll clean up here.'

'What happens next... with the Mandragora, I mean?'

Never you mind,' snapped Julian.

Creighton picked up 'Monty's' carcass and shuffled out to the van. Julian carefully placed the plant onto the stone floor, picked up a garden rake and gently turned over the disturbed soil where the Mandragora had grown. He heard the van drive away and breathed a sigh of relief. He was almost there, he congratulated himself. The hard graft was almost done, now it was time for the laboratory work to begin. Looking around to make sure that all was in order and that no indication of what went on was evident, he took up the plant and the book and carried them outside.

Dawn was just beginning to break as he unlocked the door to the laboratory.

'Good morning, sir.'

Julian spun around; the tome fell from his grasp. The security guard was on his rounds. He leaned over, picked up the book and handed it to Julian.

'Morning,' muttered Julian.

'Everything all right, sir?' the guard was looking down at the plant.

'Oh, a casualty, I'm afraid. I must find out what went wrong.'

The guard reached out and turned over one of the leaves. 'Looks like potato blight to me, sir.'

'Thank you...?'

'Fraser, sir.'

'Thank you, Fraser. Potato blight. I'll bear that in mind.'

Julian entered the lab and closed the door behind him. From the window he watched the security guard continue on his rounds, waited until he had disappeared from view and got down to work. He opened the Hermeticum Praxis, found the chapter that dealt with simulacrum and studied it for a few minutes. Next, he lay the Mandragora on the bench and, with a scalpel, sliced off four slivers of the root. He then transferred the plant carefully to a deep freeze cabinet. Returning to the bench, he placed the slivers into a pestle and ground them with a mortar. He added a few drops of distilled water until the paste became a liquid which he drew up into a pipette and transferred to a Microfuge test tube. He held the tube up against the early morning light streaming in through the window. A murky grey liquid splashed around inside. Julian crossed the lab and switched on the newly installed Isopycnic Centrifuge machine, placed the test tube in one of the special receiving bays and closed the lid. He then took a small notebook from his pocket and worked out some calculations. After checking and double-checking the figures for the speed and time required, he touched in the numbers on the digital display of the centrifuge. A sweat broke out on his forehead, his hands were sticky, he wiped them on his lab coat and pressed the start button. The machine whirred into action. He stepped back and waited.

This, for Julian, was the difficult part, waiting. Convinced of his own consummate ability, he was impatient when other agencies had to do their part, even mechanical ones. For exactly seven-minutes and twenty-three seconds he watched and waited. At last, the machine slowed down, then stopped. Julian opened the lid and took out the test tube. Once again, he held it up to the light. The liquid was now an opaque milky colour. He pulled the stopper on the test tube and, again, using a pipette, transferred a drop of the solution onto a glass slide which he placed under the electron microscope. He placed his eye to the eyepiece, made a few adjustments to the focus and studied the results. There was movement. Tiny organisms darting to and fro. He adjusted the lens and went in closer. After a minute or two he sat up straight, an elated look on his face. It had worked. A fanatical gleam came into his eyes. He, Julian Hawkes, pariah of the scientific establishment, had created life. And he recalled his mother's nickname for him when he was a child: 'Geb', God of the earth.

Chapter 8

Julian sat on the sofa. He was feeling very pleased with himself. It was nine o'clock at night and outside it was raining. Alice came in from the kitchen carrying two large glasses of white wine. She was wearing a silk gown over her negligee and high-heeled slippers. 'There. I wasn't long, was I?' She sat down next to him; they touched glasses and drank.

'You all right, Jules? You seem on edge, like you had something to tell me.'

'How long have we been together, Alice?'

Her face clouded over. *That sort of question could only lead to one conclusion,* she thought. But he was ahead of her and quickly added, 'Don't worry, Alice. I'm not going to dump you.'

The cloud lifted. 'Eleven years, three months, and nineteen days. I've got it all written down.'

He hadn't expected this. 'Written down?'

'In my diary. I began it just after you... 'rescued me'.'

Julian was alarmed by this piece of news, but he showed no sign of panic. He had planned a quiet drink, they would go to bed and make love and then, when she was satisfied and unsuspecting, he would... but her admission threw a rather large spanner into the works. 'A diary? Why you cunning little... I'd love to see it.'

'I bet you would.' She smiled that captivating smile of hers, the one that had first attracted him.

'Don't you trust me?' he asked as innocently as possible.

'It's my insurance policy. In case you get any... funny ideas.'

'Ideas? Such as?'

'Oh, trading me in for a younger model.'

He laughed. 'Clever girl.'

'I think so.' She took a sip of her wine and fixed him with a challenging stare.

'And where do you keep this 'insurance policy'?'

'Close by. Would you like to see it?' Before he could answer she rose and went into the bedroom. He had to act quickly. He drained his glass of wine. Alice returned carrying a small desk diary with a flowery cover. She handed it to him. 'Another glass?'

'Yes, please.' In the few moments she was in the kitchen refilling his glass, he deftly took a small sachet out of his top pocket and poured the contents, the same powder Creighton had used on Archie Brasher-Courtney, into her glass. He opened the diary at random. 'Did we really do that on the thirteenth of November, two years ago? he called out.

She returned, giggled, and placed his glass on the coffee table.

He turned the page. 'I see there are details of other liaisons?' He knew that he wasn't her only lover, that she carried on affairs with other men. It was Alice's way of asserting her independence. He wasn't jealous but he considered the impact should the diary fall into the wrong hands. 'Perhaps you'd like to think about what you are going to write down under today's date?'

She giggled again and took the diary from him. He smiled his most seductive smile and picked up his glass.

'Cheers. To a long and lasting relationship.' He took a drink and planted a kiss on her lips.

'You devil...' She picked up her glass and finished off her wine. 'But first,' she waved the diary in his face and returned to the bedroom.

Julian waited, a smug look on his face.

Suddenly, there was a noise, as if a table had been knocked over, and then the unmistakable sound of a body hitting the floor.

He got up and walked into the bedroom. The bureau lid was open, the bedside table was on the floor, the diary next to it. Julian picked up Alice's body and deposited her on the bed. He checked to make sure she was completely unconscious, lifting both eyelids, before preparing the operating table. He lifted her negligee, spread open her legs, and raised them slightly by bending her knees. From his pocket he took a pair of surgical gloves and put them on. Next, a syringe and a small flask containing the opaque, milky liquid that he had produced in his laboratory. He drew the liquid into the syringe, climbed onto the bed, inserted the syringe into Alice's vagina, and released the fluid. He then rearranged her legs, pulled down her negligee and tucked her under the covers. Completely unconscious, she slept on, her heavy breaths the only sound in the room.

Julian picked up the diary and the lamp and restored everything to its neat and tidy state. He went into the living room, picked up the wine glasses, took them into the kitchen and washed them both thoroughly. One he placed in the cabinet, the other he carried, along with the wine bottle, into the bedroom. He half-filled the glass and placed it on the bedside table and then splashed some of the wine onto Alice's negligee. He then carefully poured the rest down her throat, making sure that she was sitting up so as not to choke her. She gulped, coughed, then continued breathing heavily. He threw the empty bottle on the carpeted floor. What to do with the diary? He weighed it in his hands before thrusting it into a pocket. He would explain its absence at a future date. But he stopped at the front door and hesitated. Supposing Alice panicked when she realised her diary had gone? She would know that he had taken it and might act irrationally. He returned to the bedroom, took out the diary and splashed wine over as many pages as he could, and watched as the entries smudged and smeared. Then he threw it on the floor near the wine bottle. 'A calculated risk,' he told himself.

It had all gone to plan, a hastily arranged plan admittedly, but he congratulated himself on his quick thinking. He left the flat knowing that Alice would be woken in the morning by the lady who 'did for her' and that she would have a sore head. She would be initially angry but would soon calm down knowing that they had a date in two weeks' time, which gave him enough time to prepare his next move.

A few days later, in the laboratory, Julian was going over some notes he had made when Doctor Speelman entered. He was clearly embarrassed, and Julian sensed that bad news was coming.

'Professor... I've heard from California. They regard the results of your trials on the rats as... well, interesting.' Julian bristled. He had been here before. In the end, no matter how much 'freedom' is granted, it all boils down to economics.

Speelman continued, 'They will continue funding our program here as long as we steer clear of anything...'

'Controversial?' Julian finished the sentence for him.

'You know I never interfere in the way you run your department, Professor, but, from now on, if you could stay within our research guidelines.'

'If the boundaries are not pushed, science will stagnate, Doctor.'

'I understand what you are saying, believe me, but we are not a charity. Our funds are limited and are dependent on the political goodwill of various agencies, none of whom are willing to take unnecessary risks.   These are febrile times, Professor Hawkes. Animal Rights, Ethical watchdogs at every turn.'

Julian drew himself up to his full height, just as he always did when confronted with attempts to in his genius. 'How disappointing, Doctor Speelman. Just like all the others.'

Speelman shuffled his feet awkwardly.

'I may have to reconsider my position.' Julian turned away. In fact, he had already reconsidered his position. With his 'experiment' well under way he was looking forward to continuing away from the prying eyes of official supervision.

Doctor Speelman left the lab just as Creighton entered. They exchanged perfunctory glances.

'What's up with Herr Doctor?' asked Creighton. Julian ignored him and walked over to the deep freeze. He lifted the lid and stared down at the Mandragora plant, stiff and apparently lifeless.

'What are you going to do with it?' Creighton's sneering tone came at him. 'We went to a lot of trouble. I   went to a lot of trouble!'

Julian turned to face his fractious assistant. 'Not found the body, have they?' Creighton shook his head. 'And the dog?'

Again, a shake of the head.

'Then you've nothing to worry about.'

'Me? What about you? We're in this together, don't forget?'

Julian was as cool as he was methodical. 'Not long to go now, Creighton. Hold your nerve.' He knew that   Creighton was becoming a loose cannon. As long as the money and small amounts of white powder kept coming the anxious young man could be held in check, until… No, he had other concerns. Namely Alice and what he had in store for her. The difficult part, once again, was going to be the waiting. Nine months, and in that time he would have to keep her compliant until the birth. There was no doubt in his mind that she would conceive, she was healthy, despite drinking too much, she was tough, and she was smart, the diary proved that.

That evening he and Joan played whist together.

'You seem in rather a good mood, husband.'

'Do I? Well, I was going to tell you. I had some good news today. The trials on the genetic makeup of the albino rats raised a few eyebrows in California.'

'That's marvellous, Jules.'

'Yes. Doctor Speelman has given me the go-ahead to continue experimenting'. He was a very convincing liar. 'It does mean that I shall be away from home a fair bit over the next few months.'

She was very understanding, and they arranged to have Mrs Crafford come and live in and be a companion to Joan.

Alice had indeed woken the following morning with a sore head. Her 'maid' had disposed of the empty bottle of wine and been very discreet about how she had found her mistress. It was not the first time. She was upset about the state of her diary and not convinced that it had been entirely her fault. She recalled the evening with Julian but not that she had drunk too much. Still, she reasoned, if he had been at all worried about her 'insurance policy' he would have taken it with him and destroyed it.

When, three weeks later, her doctor confirmed her pregnancy, Alice was at first dismayed then a sense of well-being took hold of her, as if she was now the complete woman. She knew Julian was the father, she'd had no other flings for some time. Now, perhaps, she thought, he would become more of a partner, no more sneaking off in the early hours, no more unannounced visits, or impromptu calls.

When she broke the news to Julian, he convincingly feigned surprise and immediately took on the role of caring father. The matter of the diary was conveniently forgotten. In fact, he had bought her an expensive new diary to replace the damaged one. He arranged a refuge away from London in Northampton, explaining that he knew a reputable obstetrician who worked at a private hospital in the town. Also, it was closer to Cambridge, and he would be able to visit more often. Alice settled into her new home contentedly. She took her medication, iron pills and vitamin supplements, took daily walks and prepared for her new role in life.

Julian did indeed visit often, sometimes staying for days at a time.

After seven months, an extraordinary stroke of luck gave Julian the opportunity he was looking for. He hadn't quite worked out how he was going to separate mother and child without causing disquiet. And then Alice was rushed into the private hospital and, after a very difficult confinement and a caesarean section—she nearly died—gave birth to a premature baby, a girl. The baby stayed on life support, and, after a few weeks, Alice was allowed home. Julian took charge. With his considerable wealth and with the help of a disreputable private detective who owed him a favour, he oiled a few palms and had the infant's name registered as Alana, and then immediately began adoption procedures, claiming that the mother, a former prostitute, was unfit to care for the child. While the adoption papers were being processed, he cared for Alice. A diet of white wine combined with a morphine-based pain-killer and various other dubious substances rendered her completely dependent on him. She put on weight and was confined to her bed until Julian cancelled the lease on the Northampton residence and took her back to Belgravia. 'Familiar surrounding will help your recovery,' she had been told and in her befuddled state she was in no position to argue.

Chapter 9

Julian sat on the bed holding her hand. 'I know we talked about it, and I know that I didn't want anything to get in the way of my work.'

'But Julian…' He interrupted her. 'I know what you're going to say. Our age. But it's all fine. All the checks and tests of suitability have been made. Everything has been arranged.'

'Oh, Julian. How old is she?

'Newborn'.

'A daughter…' Tears welled up in Joan's eyes and she clasped Julian's hand to her lips. 'A companion for you to play card games with,' he joked.

She was speechless with joy and gratitude. They were going to be a family at last.

As he left her bedroom, he reflected that it was strange how tender he could be with Joan in contrast with his treatment of Alice. But he didn't allow himself to entertain the notion for long. After all, it had been a noted characteristic of his that once someone was of no use he discarded them - like Alice, and soon, Creighton.

In his study he gazed at the painting of 'The Alchemist' and compared himself to the bearded ancient. 'The means justified the ends,' Professor Meinengen had convinced him, adding that the only goal was scientific progress, and nothing should stand in its way. And nothing did. He, Julian Hawkes, had become a modern-day alchemist. Looking down he noticed that several faxes were hanging out of the machine and his telephone answering machine was flashing with messages. His mobile phone indicated the same. He ignored them, left the study, and walked down the corridor towards the laboratory. He entered, switched on the light, and viewed the space with some disquiet. Since he had commenced his job at the Davos Foundation the place had become rather dilapidated. The deep freeze was ten years old, what equipment there was had a layer of dust. It needed a refit. He thought about surreptitiously 'borrowing' a few items—a centrifuge, an electron microscope—from Davos but rejected the idea. Security had been stepped up. Julian noticed that Fraser, the security guard whom he had befriended, had been replaced by a set of guards from another company. Also, a gardener had been employed to look after, not only the grounds, but the hot house as well. Julian knew that the writing was on the wall.

And sure enough, a few weeks later, he was summoned to Doctor Speelman's office. Julian stood with his back to Doctor Speelman looking out over the carefully manicured grounds of the Davos Foundation. The new gardener was busy at work tending a flower bed. The Doctor was contrite. 'Believe me, Julian, I pleaded with them, I begged them to let you continue... but we must face facts. Times have changed, research is changing. Scientific Foundations like Davos must take ethical factors into consideration.' He shuffled a few papers on his desk and continued. 'I don't need to remind you that, as stated in your contract with us, all research materials and findings are the sole property of the Foundation.'

Julian stormed out of the office. Back in the laboratory he ignored Creighton's greeting and opened the deep freeze. There was his creation, literally 'on ice'. He wasn't going to let go of the

Mandragora. The albino rats, everything else they could keep. Plans to steal it were already forming in his mind.

One of the new security guards entered the laboratory alongside Doctor Speelman. Creighton accepted his letter of dismissal with meek submission. Julian refused to take his. He turned his back, folded his arms, and stared fixedly out of the window. The Doctor placed the letter on the work bench, mumbled a pathetic, 'I'm sorry', and left.

'Keys, Professor Hawkes,' the security guard demanded. Julian handed them over and left. As Creighton tamely gave up the key to the van, he heard the sound of his master's sports car as it roared away and after he had left the premises two workmen entered the laboratory and fixed a padlock to the deep freeze.

That same evening, as Creighton was contemplating his precarious situation over a joint and a can of beer, there was a knock at his front door. It was Julian. He threw an envelope on the table. 'You'll need that... now that you're unemployed.' Creighton opened the envelope, took out the wad of cash and the small sachet.

'We've another job to do.'

'Not me. I'm finished. With the lab, with murder, with you.'

Julian grabbed him by his shirt collar and pushed him up against the wall. He knew the day would come when he would have to again play rough with his assistant. 'Listen. One word from me and you'll go down for Archie's murder. Do you think for one moment anyone would believe you if you told them the whole story? Do you think the police, lawyers, a jury would believe that Professor Julian Hawkes could get himself involved with an ex-drug addict with a criminal record?' He let go of Creighton who stumbled back against the wall. He was frightened but not to the extent that he didn't realise that what his

Master had said made sense. Who would believe him? The irony was that, in a small way, he was grateful to Julian for rescuing him from a life of dissipation, for giving him back a purpose in life. Admittedly it was a sinister one, but he had discovered hidden depths to his character, and he was materially better off than he had ever been. No, he would have to bide his time, go along with the 'mad professor' until the time was right, and he could make his move.

A few weeks earlier, in anticipation of his dismissal from Davos, Julian had had two duplicate keys made—one to the laboratory and one to the conservatory. It was the latter that, a couple of hours after the confrontation with Creighton, Julian used to enter the greenhouse. Creighton followed carrying a wooden box. They noiselessly moved over the stone floor and stopped at the bed where the Mandrake plant had grown. The patch of earth was still bare, nothing had been planted in its place.

'I couldn't get anything to grow there, after...' whispered Creighton.

'You wouldn't. It's dead ground.'

Julian had brought the small trowel with which he dug a square around the patch of barren soil. He carefully, almost reverentially, lifted it into the box. 'Take that back to the car and wait for me,' said Julian. 'I have one more visit to make.'

They had parked a mile or so away from the Foundation and entered the grounds through some disused farm buildings that bordered the site.

Creighton went off with the now heavier wooden box while Julian made his way towards the laboratory. Using the other duplicate key, he entered and crossed to the deep freeze. He was at first surprised then angered when he saw the padlock. But fury only intensified his efforts. Using a pair of tongs and a utility clamp he eventually managed to break the lock. He took a large freezer bag from his coat pocket, opened it out and, with great care, slid the plant inside. Locking the door behind him he disappeared into the darkness, never to be seen at the Davos Foundation again.

'You took your time. I was beginning to think they'd nabbed you.'

'Doctor Speelman was clever,' said Julian as he transferred the freezer bag into a large plastic drum packed with ice. 'But not clever enough to outwit me.' Creighton raised his eyes. He had heard it all before, the boosterism, the self-congratulatory tone. As Julian started the car he cried out, 'now, the work continues!'

Julian dropped Creighton off close to his house. It was three in the morning. 'Any word of this and…'

'I know,' interrupted the young man sardonically, 'you will make my life a misery.' He slammed the door and marched away. Julian frowned. He needed Creighton for one more task, the riskiest of all, and there were no alternatives. For the time being he had to keep him compliant. He drove off and arrived back at the Mendes House just as dawn was breaking.

As quietly as he could, Julian removed the wooden box from the boot and carried it into the laboratory. Next, he brought in the plastic drum. He placed it on the bench and removed the lid. The Mandragora lay there, ice cold, fresh and ready to be regenerated. Julian couldn't wait. He was tired but sleep would have to wait. From a drawer he took the ancient tome, the Hermeticum Praxis, and opened it at the relevant page. Standing on the bench was a large glass observation chamber, newly purchased. It had a temperature gauge which he adjusted before continuing. He slid up one side and removed the glass. Using the trowel, he relocated the dead soil from the wooden box into a large clay pot. When he was satisfied, he lifted the Mandragora out of the freezer bag and carefully replanted it. He added a few drops of distilled water, a dash of liquid fertiliser, moved the pot and plant into the chamber, replaced the glass and stood back.

He consulted the text again, then looked up impatiently. *Perhaps I should come back later, give it time to bed in,* he thought. But then, as if responding to his thoughts, the plant reacted. Its leaves, frozen until now, threw off their icy glaze and slowly quivered into verdant life. The main stem seemed to grow another few centimetres as it regained its former robust appearance. Julian was amazed at the transformation which had taken place. But then, he wasn't surprised at all. The ancients knew a thing or two. It was all in the book. He had scrupulously followed the instructions and the results were there, in front of him. The same results as would have been reached in days gone by. Exultant, he closed the lab and retired to bed.

A week later the 'Mother Plant', as Julian had come to regard it, was in rude health and it held pride of place in the laboratory. Although in a chamber which was isolated from the atmosphere—specially filtered air was pumped in—it seemed to have extra-sensory life, moving with Julian as he passed by, reacting to the fluctuating light sources. One day, intrigued by its behaviour, Julian stood in front of the glass case and watched as the plant seemed to react to his presence by moving in a sensual way, gently writhing, leaves trembling. Was it aware of a human presence and if so, was it interacting in a friendly manner… or was it frightened? He consulted the pages of the tome but could find no information to explain the strange activity.

'What do you do down there all day and night, Julian?' The question was rhetorical. He was about to reply when interrupted by the sound of Alana crying. Alana, now three months old, had been installed in the nursery in the room next to Joan's. A nurse had been in attendance for a short time until Joan got the hang of things and aided by Mrs Crafford, a 'baby-friendly' routine was soon in full sway.

'It's Alana's feed time,' said Joan. Mrs Crafford appeared with the baby, and she passed the infant into Joan's arms. She slid her nightdress down from her shoulder, bared her breast and gently brought the child's mouth into contact with her nipple. Despite his absences, Julian had become aware of how the whole experience of mothering had affected his wife. Joan was the happiest she had ever been, her complexion was more vivid, she had regained energy and purpose, she even seemed to be younger.

One evening after Alana had been put to bed and Mrs Crafford had gone home, Joan outlined to Julian all the plans she had for their daughter; private school, university, a well-paid job, perhaps in journalism or broadcasting, a good marriage and then grandchildren for her and Julian to enjoy in their old age. Julian humoured her, went along with her fantasy, having already made his own plans for Alana's future.

During this time, when he wasn't in his laboratory, Julian made regular visits to Alice in Belgravia. He needed to keep her in the soporific state to which she had been induced. Occasionally, when she remembered, she asked after her baby. Julian explained that it was still very ill due to the pre-term birth, but he knew that he couldn't keep up the pretense for long, and, after a few weeks he admitted, 'She's been put up for adoption.'

Alice was distraught. She attacked him, accused him of vile offences against her body. 'Anyway...' she blurted out, 'you're not the father. I lied to you when I said I hadn't slept with any other men.' He was forced to administer a strong dose of a sleeping draught. As he dragged her into her bed, he considered that there was a paradox here. Supposing she had had intercourse with another and the sperm from Archie Brasher-Courtney had mixed with… a lesser being! Well, it was too late now, and, in his arrogant way, he dismissed the idea. He called the doctor he had engaged, an elderly ex-member of the profession who had been struck off for dabbling in dubious practices, and explained that Alice had, once again, become irrational and unreasonable and would he come round.

As he drove away from Belgravia and into Park Lane, he troubled himself by reflecting on how much all this was costing; the flat, the doctor, the pills, the booze. It was time, he told himself, to bring this sordid side of his life to a close.

The next night, he visited Creighton at his home. The place was becoming untidy again; empty beer cans, pizza boxes, clothes strewn about, the kitchen sink piled with dirty crockery. There were dark rings around Creighton's eyes, he was thinner, haggard looking.

'Just as Davos let us both go, Creighton, now I'm letting you go. But I have that one last job for you. I want you to go to an address in London and I want you to dispose of the woman who lives there. I don't care how, but make it look good… like we did with that student.' Subtlety wasn't Julian's style. His imposing, fanatical presence filled the room.

Creighton looked at him with an uneasy mixture of slavish duty and truculence. 'I told you. I'm all done with murder.'

Julian produced a large manila envelope from his coat and lay it on the coffee table. 'There's enough in there for you to start again, twice over. But away from here. Do you understand?'

Creighton, suspicious, opened the envelope and peered inside. A very thick wad of large denomination bank notes was inside, along with the inevitable sachet of white powder.

'You could begin a new life, abroad if you wished. In fact, I think abroad would be best for all concerned.'

Creighton began to count the money. 'Very generous of you, Professor.'

Julian pressed home his advantage. 'What's another murder to you? And this time it's someone you don't know and who doesn't know you. No motive. The perfect crime.'

Creighton's acquisitive nature had got the upper hand. He couldn't believe what looked like an enormous amount of money, and all in used notes. His surly manner gradually changed.

Julian, noting his ex-assistant's demeanour, leaned closer, and in a threatening manner said, 'Because if you ever come into my life again, I shall surely kill you.'

A small dent was made in Julian's inducement when Creighton bought himself a second-hand car, a white Ford Cortina. And a few days later he drove to London and parked in a side street in Belgravia. It was eleven-thirty at night and raining steadily. He looked at the piece of paper that Julian had handed him, and which bore the address, neatly typed out, of the flat. Creighton steeled himself, after all, as Julian had pointed out, what's another murder? He checked that the street was empty of pedestrians, and that no security cameras were pointing his way, climbed out of the car, locked it, and hurried across the road and into the mews.

He was about to ring the bell when the front door opened and a shabbily dressed elderly man emerged, brushed past him in a furtive manner, head down, and dashed away wrestling with his umbrella as he went. Creighton caught the door before it closed, entered, and climbed the stairs.

Alice had let herself go further. She was in a permanently dazed state. Her dressing gown, once elegant, was drab and tattered. The flat was untidy. Julian had let the maid go. Alice had taken to seeing one or two of her old customers, a decision that Julian was angry about. But what could he do? If it kept her mind off 'things', he reasoned, all the better.

Creighton stood in the living room. The sound of a bottle being opened came from the kitchen. His presence, unannounced startled Alice and she almost dropped her drink. 'Who are you? How d'ye get in?'

'The door was open,' he replied.

'You're new. Not one of my regulars.' She flopped down on the sofa.

'A mutual friend recommended you.'

'Oh? Well, as long as you can pay.' Her mood brightened. 'Come and join me. Get yourself a drink. In the kitchen.'

Creighton sat down next to her. 'No, thank you.'

'Suit yourself.' She peered at him through her bleary eyes. 'My, you're young... for your age.' She giggled and took a sip of wine.

'This friend, he said that you were very accommodating.'

'Always nice to hear a compliment. You don't have to tell me his name. Not if it might be compromising. I mean, I have lots of clients in, shall we say, sensitive positions, so I understand if you don't want to mention your friend's name.'

'I don't mind telling you. Professor Julian Hawkes.'

Alice started and spilt some wine on her gown. For a moment she almost sobered up. 'Who are you? What do you want?'

Creighton took a deep breath, then, in as calm a voice as he could muster, he said, 'Well. It's rather awkward. You see... I've come to kill you.'

Chapter 10

Julian was in his study, drinking a glass of whisky. He was privately celebrating the termination of his connections to both Alice and Creighton. All he had asked of his former assistant was that, when the deed had been done, he take himself off and send a postcard with the simple message, 'Wish you were here.' That November morning, six months to the day from his final encounter with Creighton, the postcard had arrived. The stamp indicated Spain. He afforded himself a wry smile. He had been very fond of Alice, he briefly consoled himself with the memory of her welcoming arms, but scientific progress had to be made.

The late-night news was on the television, and he sat up when Maurice Bond appeared outside the Houses of Parliament airing his views on the Governments latest education plans. There had been a few points of contact since their initial meeting but nothing substantial had come of them. It was a pity. Since paying off Creighton, the private detective in Northampton, the doctor in Belgravia and various other 'helpful people' funds were running low. No publishers wanted his articles any more and the world of academia had firmly closed its doors. While he mused on his parlous state the telephone rang.

'Julian Hawkes? Maurice Bond here.' *What a coincidence,* thought Julian. But then he half-believed in such events. The Hermeticum Praxis had taught him that.

'More idle blather,' was what Julian expected and he sat back. But no. It appeared that 'talks' had progressed and that he,

Maurice, was in a position to make an offer. He proposed that they drive up to the 'Mendes House' that evening. *They,* thought Julian? 'It must be serious,' and he hung up, went upstairs, and explained to Joan that he was expecting late night visitors and not to be alarmed.

At about midnight, a very shiny black car pulled up on the gravel drive. The chauffeur opened the rear door and two men got out. Maurice was accompanied by a tall, middle-aged man, who had a patrician air about him. Julian met them at the front door and took them into the study.

'This is Gordon Macdonald; he works for to the Treasury department.'

Julian shook his hand.

'I'm sorry for the late and sudden intrusion but after our last meeting I thought…'

The Treasury man was taking an interest in the oil painting, 'The Alchemist' and peered at it studiously.

'Are you interested in art or alchemy?' asked Julian.

'Neither, actually,' he answered in a non-committal public school way.

'I asked Gordon along so that you can see that we are serious about… things.'

'Yes, I was wondering if this was an official visit,' said Julian.

'If you mean, are Gordon and me authorised, well, no. But you mustn't be concerned,' he hastily added.

The Treasury man turned away from the painting. 'We are here with the sanction of a very powerful group within the cabinet.'

Julian was suspicious. He had been courted by well-meaning 'officialdom' too many times in the past, all leading to disappointment, to let it happen again.

Maurice sat down in a leather armchair, but he was clearly on edge. 'As you know, Professor Hawkes... er, may I call you Julian?

Julian didn't respond.

'The pressures on ministerial budgets are severe. Ways must be found to deliver maximum serviceability at an affordable cost.'

Julian had heard it all before but gave nothing away.

'And sometimes... we have to think outside the box,' Maurice continued.

'Cliches, a convenient refuge for the unimaginative, were starting', thought Julian. He noticed that Maurice was beginning to sweat again. 'When were they going to get to the point?'

Eventually, after more cliches, mixed metaphors and political gobbledygook, Maurice took a deep breath and spoke. 'Our brief is to make available to you, funding that would let you continue the research program that was curtailed two years ago.'

There was an awkward silence. *Go on,* thought Julian, *let's hear the actual words.*

Maurice blurted out, 'Your social engineering program.'

Maurice, much relieved, settled back into the chair. Julian didn't react, waiting for the inevitable 'if's', but's' and conditions. Gordon MacDonald broke his silence. 'We have people looking at a more friendly profile for what has become, wrongly in our view, a disreputable discipline.'

'Of course. You'd have to,' said Julian.

'After all, if people are going to be won over...' He stressed the word 'people' as if they were an unavoidable nuisance. Julian made a point of appearing indifferent and he started to sort through his faxes.

Maurice quickly realised that the matter of remuneration had to be broached. 'To the tune of half a million   pounds a year.' Julian turned. His urbane manner cloaked the agitation within, and he quickly made up his mind to accept but he decided to play hard to get. 'Social engineering is a wide and varied field.'

Maurice took another deep breath. 'Specifically, eugenics.'

There was a long silence during which Julian refilled his glass of whisky. 'Can I offer you gentlemen...'

'No, thank you. We must get back to London.' Maurice stood up. 'But our people must have an answer soon.'

'Conditions,' said Julian.

'No e-mails. No written exchanges. No phone or text communication.'

'Nothing a snoopy journalist could get his hands on,' added MacDonald, again the sneering tone.   'And we don't need, or want, to know your methods, just the results.'

'You realise that a program like this will take time, perhaps years?'

'Then, I take it, you're on board?' presumed the man from the Treasury.

'When the first payment is in my bank,' he scrawled down the details of his private bank on a piece of paper, 'I shall begin work.' He handed over the paper. 'Don't forget to destroy that,' he added with a wry smile on his lips.

After they had gone, Julian toasted the Alchemist in the painting. He hadn't admitted to the Men from the Ministry that he had already started on his own eugenics project. That the first yield of his research was asleep in her cot just above their heads. How clever he was. Now, with proper funding and absolute freedom he could press on. The rehabilitation of Professor Julian Hawkes into the lofty heights of scientific immortality was about to commence.

Chapter 11

The money appeared in Julian's bank account a week later. He had sweated a bit when there was no sign of any activity and initially put it down to bureaucracy but then speculated that the money probably wouldn't have come through official channels and so he decided to check up. After much bureaucratic wrangling with his bank, he found out that the payment had been made by a clearing bank in Switzerland. He got his bank to send him a copy of the cheque and it had a stamp overlay from an account in the Channel Islands. The signature was almost indecipherable but after close examination through a magnifying glass Julian made out a name, 'Bracho'. He went onto the internet, and after a labyrinthine search, found a company of that name listed as a Hedge Fund in California with a subsidiary on the Cayman Islands. He was satisfied that his midnight visitors had been as good as their word and that the clandestine nature of the operation was justified.

Julian had told Joan of his good fortune but was suitably vague. 'A sort of government post, but it means I can work at home.' As he predicted, Joan was too absorbed with Alana to take much notice and the matter was not mentioned again. Mrs Crafford still came in to help but she and Julian hardly crossed paths as he was caught up with his work.

The refurbishment of the laboratory was first on the agenda. It had originally been a storage room with only one entrance from inside the house. Julian had another door put in that opened directly onto the back garden and, on the stone patio, a large hot house was built with the most up-to-date temperature control, venting and sprinkler systems. Soon to follow was the laboratory and after extensive restructuring and modernisation looked every bit the equal, if not the better, of the Davos lab. It was fitted out with all the latest high-tech equipment—centrifuges, electronic microscopes, spectrometers, plate readers, homogenisers, cryocampact circulators, cryogenic refrigerators, etc., all connected digitally to a series of laptop computers. Cages were installed in a large corrugated shed in the back garden, just beyond the new hot house, to house the animals he needed for his experiments.

Next on the agenda was a classroom for Alana. He was certain that home-instruction was best for her. Because of the nature of her 'origins' he couldn't risk any awkward questions that might arise in the heated atmosphere of a regular school. Initially, Joan wasn't happy with Julian's plan for their daughter but with the argument that this way she would spend more time at home, he gradually won her over.

Julian had one of the downstairs rooms that had become a junk room converted, complete with blackboard, charts, maps, a bench with Bunsen burner and microscope, numerous textbooks, and study guides. He also found a copy of 'Arrowsmith', the book that had inspired him, and placed it proudly on the bookshelf. A single desk occupied the centre of the room.

As Alana reached her second year her precocity was more than evident, and, on the retirement of Mrs Crafford, a nanny was engaged. She didn't quite reach Julian's high standards—she had come from an agency and was used to doing things 'her way'— and was followed by a succession of au-pairs' and governesses all of whom, much to Joan's exasperation, fell short of the mark, or rather Julian's impossibly high standards.

By the time of Alana's fifth birthday Julian assumed full control and instruction began in earnest. Joan had indeed raised an eyebrow when Julian had outlined his plan, but she still trusted him. Her only concern was that would he still have time to carry on with his own work and she persuaded him to bring in private tutors for certain areas of Alana's education. Reluctantly he agreed. He was not musical or of a sporting bent so, after meticulous vetting, a series of instructors were engaged. A piano teacher came in twice a week, riding lessons were provided in a paddock that had been created on a plot of land behind the house, a tennis court had been constructed and a coach engaged for lessons three times a week.

Julian took care of her formal studies, and it soon became clear that Alana was very bright. She didn't need to be told anything twice, her mind was like a sponge, absorbing anything and everything that Julian placed before her. The first significant moment came during an English lesson with a quote, scrawled on the blackboard, from 'Alice in Wonderland', *Speak English! I don't know the meaning of half those long words, and I don't believe you do either!'*

'Write down and comprehend, please,' he instructed Alana.

Sitting at the desk, her black hair falling over her shoulders, the skinny child copied the words into an exercise book. When she had finished, she looked up. Her face had a curious blank expression as if it was inviting knowledge and experience to enter.

'Well? What do you make of that, Alana?'

She put down her book and pencil and stepped up to the blackboard, took a piece of chalk, and underlined the word '*English*'. At first taken aback, Julian then laughed and commended her perspicacity. He relayed the incident to Joan that evening.

'Then, perhaps Alana would be good at languages?' Joan said. He hadn't thought of it but followed up on her suggestion and by the time Alana was fifteen she had mastered French, Latin, Spanish, Russian and German and had a working grasp of a dozen other languages.

A major part of Alana's education was, of course, in the sciences, in particular biology. When she was five years old, Julian introduced her to Aristotle's four ancient elements.

Firstly, he produced a small flowerpot containing soil. 'Earth.' He dug his fingers in and invited Alana to do the same. She touched the earth tentatively then as the soil felt warm and inviting, she pushed her small hand in. She repeated the word, 'earth.'

Next, he turned the tap on and invited her to wash her fingers. 'Water.' They both rinsed their hands under the running water. She seemed to be enjoying this lesson.

Then, Julian took a deep breath and swiped his arm in a curve through the air. 'Air.' Alana copied him, 'Air,' and described a smaller arc.

Lastly, he struck a match and set off the Bunsen burner; the flame shot up. 'Fire!' he exclaimed. But Alana's reaction was to recoil, almost falling off her stool. 'Don't be frightened,' he urged. But she was genuinely terrified. Julian turned down the flame to its lowest point. He watched her closely, after all she was not only his stepdaughter but was his experiment as well. She quickly recovered but was forever wary of the naked flame.

The only subject not on Julian's curriculum was religious study. They touched on it as part of history—it was impossible not to—but bible and faith studies were deemed irrelevant. Julian was to be the only 'god' in Alana's universe.

One day, when she was six years old, he had allowed Alana to visit his laboratory. She was curious as to where her father went to work. He unlocked the door and led her inside. She wandered around, looking at the equipment and the various test-tubes and flasks with strange, coloured liquids and the substances in them.

The glass jars containing preserved animal parts she found particularly interesting but, strangely, she didn't seem as interested in the live animals, at least not in the way a girl of her age should have been. He took a squirrel monkey out of its cage and presented it to her, but she just looked at it in a curious way before moving on. As she walked past the chamber containing the 'Mother Plant' Julian noticed that the leaves trembled, the stems seemed to lean towards her as if they recognised something in her. Of course, they would, he reasoned. It was a revealing moment for Julian. He now had living proof that genetic mutation between human and non-human cells was a viable proposition.

During this time, as Alana grew into a teenager, Julian had not been neglecting his other experiments. Cut sections from the 'Mother Plant' had been stored in the deep freeze and were used in various tests and trials. The hot house in the garden had become home to a thriving community of Mandragora specimens. Julian was in the greenhouse one day, watering the plants and removing any dead stock, when Alana walked past on her way to the tennis court. The plants were suddenly stimulated, tracking her motion as she went by, subsiding after she had disappeared. Julian was again fascinated but not surprised. He kept a log of all the results of his tests and trials and made copious notes to do with the correlation between Alana's behaviour and the Mandragora's response.

In the few quiet moments Julian allowed himself, often when Alana was hard at work on a mathematical calculation or copying a passage into her exercise book, he was given to thinking about which parent had passed on to her which trait. Alana clearly inherited her intelligence, sporting ability and good looks from both parents. Beyond that it was difficult to draw a conclusion. Did it matter, he asked himself? He was moulding her now and that is all that would count. The one area where there was slight concern was to do with her imagination. At the age of six, when he had sat her down with easel and paint, she had asked, 'What do you want me to paint?' As an infant she had hardly ever drawn in crayon or doodled idly. 'Whatever comes to mind,' was his reply. He returned an hour later to find the canvas still blank. In all other disciplines she performed each task allotted with slavish accuracy. In the laboratory when instructed to carry out the distillation of ammonia from tap water she followed the formula to the letter. Julian dismissed from his mind any notion that Alana was lacking a creative impulse. He convinced himself that her imagination would develop as she developed—after all, under his tutelage it was bound to.

It was as she turned nine that Joan expressed her concern about Alana's social life. 'She has no close friends. She's never had a birthday party. A young girl needs like-minded friends who she can talk to about girly things.' Julian brushed aside her misgivings. A far as he was concerned, she didn't need anyone, she had her father... 'and you, of course', he added.

'But it's not enough, husband,' she chided him. But, as ever, his resolve held sway.

Once a year, sometimes twice, Julian would receive a visit from Maurice Bond. It was always unannounced. 'As I was passing this way...' he would say. One windy autumn day Julian was in his study when he heard the gate being unlatched and a car on the gravel drive. Alana was having her piano lesson, the sound of a Bach fugue drifted along the passages of the Mendes House. 'My daughter,' explained Julian as he let Maurice in at the front door. The Minister's public profile had increased, he was always on the television and radio and in the newspapers. He was now a member of the Cabinet with special responsibility for Further Education. He still maintained his youthful looks and was tipped as a future party leader. 'We hadn't heard from you in some time, so I thought I'd come by,' said Maurice.

'I don't believe I thanked you for getting the school inspector off my back,' said Julian. When it became known that Alana was going to be educated at home a rather officious lady Inspector from the county school board, who obviously didn't approve, had turned up at the house. Julian had put up with her first visit but after the second, a week later, had made a private call to Maurice.

'Oh, yes. The state sector can be rather intrusive.' The interference ceased immediately.

Julian told him about the progress he had been making and showed him a few specimens in the laboratory; a genetically modified agave cactus and a hybrid albino monkey, part Macaque, part Capuchin. Maurice allowed himself to be impressed but the detailed scientific data that Julian gave out went over his head. Most of it was designed that way, Julian being reluctant to give away any secrets. 'When can I go back to my people with something more… substantial.' Maurice asked in a whisper.

'I said it might take years,' Julian replied.

'We realise that, but…'

'If you're not happy, end the thing. Cut the funding,' Julian snapped back. He was used to dealing with people in authority, knew that they revelled in the cut and thrust of heady debate.

'No, no... there's no question of that,' and he turned his attention to the distant playing of the piano. 'Very accomplished.'

'My daughter. Would you like to see?' Julian, playing the devil, decided to let the Minister, unwittingly, view his most advanced 'experiment'. The music room had been created near the bottom of the stairs so that Joan could enjoy the music. Julian and Maurice entered quietly. Alana, her back to them, moved her head side to side, her jet-black hair tossing back and forth. Julian noticed that her piano teacher, an intense looking twenty-two-year-old mature student, wasn't looking at the sheet music. His gaze was fixed intently on Alana. He looked up at the visitors and was about to halt the lesson, but Julian gestured for it to continue. As the last note faded away, Maurice clapped his hands and Alana turned.

'Maurice Bond... my daughter, Alana,' said Julian.

'Thank you. That was delightful.'

'It wasn't for you,' pointed out the seven-year-old. 'It's just today's lesson.'

Maurice was taken aback. 'Nevertheless, it was lovely.' There was an awkward silence broken by the student gathering up the sheet music and stepping away from the piano. 'Well, until next week. Alana, Professor...' He turned and left the room. Alana looked up at Maurice in the very direct way that she had cultivated. Some people found it unsettling. But Maurice was struck by Alana's looks. He perceived an ethereal quality under that steady gaze unusual for one so young.

'I've seen you on the television,' remarked Alana as she closed the piano lid and stood up.

'Mister Bond is a wielder of power and influence in high places, Alana,' explained Julian, a hint of sarcasm in his voice.

She was unmoved. 'I'm going to get a drink, father. I have twenty minutes before my riding lesson.'

Maurice watched her leave the room. He had not noticed anything unusual about her, she was just a pretty little girl to him. 'You'll have to keep an eye on that one, Julian. She's going to be a 'looker' in a few years' time.'

Julian deplored his coarse tone, led Maurice back to his car and waved him away in a dismissive manner. Thank goodness these visits were so infrequent, he reminded himself. Over the years General Elections had come and gone and the Government changed hands numerous times, but it didn't seem to affect Julian's relationship with Maurice and his paymasters. He questioned Maurice about it on one of his visits and he replied, 'You're getting paid, aren't you?' Yes, he was, handsomely, a half a million pounds dropped into his bank account on a regular basis and his work carried on.

'Who was that, came to visit?' asked Joan.

'A man from the Ministry.' He could see she was tired, and he bolstered her pillows and smoothed her duvet.

'What did he want?'

'Nothing. Just some bureaucratic red tape to clear up.'

She knew when he was being evasive. 'You used to share your work secrets with me.'

'Did I? But I don't have any secrets. My work is very mundane, wife.'

She sighed. It was useless to pry. 'I do envy you your work, husband.'

He didn't respond. He was watching from the bedroom window as Alana, astride a dun pony, jumped a series of fences. The instructor, a large middle-aged lady wearing boots and a long skirt, held one end of a rope tied to the pony's bit.

'Julian?'

He turned back to her.

'Sorry, dear. What did you say?'

'I said, our daughter plays the piano well.'

He frowned. 'Yes… But I'm worried about her teacher.'

'Oh. Why? He seems a perfectly nice young man.'

Julian was troubled and had been ever since relinquishing control, no matter how slight, to others. 'Oh, it doesn't matter. I'll deal with it. Well, I must get back to work.' He kissed her lightly on the forehead and walked out.

Ever since Alana had entered their lives, Joan had seen a change in him. He was becoming more obsessive over their daughter and less concerned with the family aspect of their lives together. It was as if he had assumed that Joan's affection for Alana would supplant her feelings for him. Jealousy was beginning to consume him. She could see it in his eyes when on occasion he would enter her bedroom and find them playing cards together. 'Join us, Julian. We can play three-handed bridge.' But he turned, stormed out and returned to his laboratory.

Joan was becoming weaker, frailer. Calling the doctor became a frequent occurrence. Various medicines were prescribed, but nothing seemed to work, and her health continued to decline. 'Really, Mister Hawkes, your wife should be in hospital,' the doctor said repeatedly. But his recommendations were ignored. Julian was in charge of the family, as he was with all aspects of life at 'The Mendes House'.

A few weeks after Maurice Bond's visit, Alana entered the music room to begin her lesson. From her bedroom, as she was dressing, she had heard her teacher, the student, enter the house a full ten minutes before, but had deliberately chosen to keep him waiting. She didn't know where this sense of prevarication had come from, and it surprised her.

Julian had also heard the front door open and close and had quickly finished dressing. He had decided that his daughter required a new teacher and this callow youth, whose looks of longing aimed at Alana had nothing to do with her musical ability, had to go.

When Alana finally did enter the music room, she found her teacher hanging by his neck from a beam in the ceiling, his body gently swaying, the rope creaking. She stood for a moment or two contemplating the scene, wondering what her reaction should be. When Julian appeared, he was as shocked as much by the appalling scene—memories of, not only his father but of Archie Brasher-Courtney, came to him—as by Alana's seeming indifference. He hustled her out of the room, locked the door and called the police.

'It's probably the shock,' said the Detective who came to the house. He was referring to Alana's apparent lack of reaction to the incident. She had agreed to answer questions and answered them with clarity and a marked lack of emotion. No, the student, whose name was Graham Keys, had never made a pass at her, had never touched her in an intimate way and had never discussed anything other than music. When the Detective asked, did she think he might have had a 'crush' on her, she looked puzzled for a moment, then, having considered what he meant, replied, 'I don't know. He might have done.' She didn't reveal that the afternoon before his demise, as she was showing him out of the house, he had turned to her and said, in a harsh, bitter voice, 'I can't go on like this. You must know...' Alana, unaware and unconcerned about his feelings, replied, 'Until tomorrow then...'

and closed the door in his face.

Julian supplied the police with information about the student, when he was engaged, his qualifications, how he had help improve his daughter's piano playing no end. The body was taken away, the police left, and Julian had the unenviable task of telling Joan what had occurred. Later that evening Alana played a hand of whist with her mother, just as she did every Wednesday evening. Joan, too, was struck by her calm manner and put it down to delayed shock.

'Twenty-seven.' Alana noted the score down on the scorecard.

'Alana? Don't you ever get tired of winning?'

'I can't seem to help it, mother,' she replied in a sweet, but strangely distant voice.

'Perhaps I'm just no good at cards,' sighed Joan.

'Another hand?' Alana began to deal and turned over a card, the nine of spades. Her mother gasped.

'What is it, mother?

Joan regained her breath and Alana, unaware of the card's sinister connotation, carried on dealing but Joan stayed her hand.

'No, I'm tired…'

Alana gathered up the cards and placed them on the bedside table. She got up to go but hesitated and sat back down again.

'Mother. What's going to become of me?'

Joan was taken aback. This was not the sort of question that her self-assured daughter had ever asked before and it was also the first time she had seemed genuinely puzzled by something.

'Why? What do you mean?'

'It's just that… what does Father plan to do with me?'

'His intentions are for the best, my darling. You must…'

'Obey him?' She finished off her mother's sentence for her.

Joan considered her response carefully, leaned forward, grasped Alana's hand, and said, 'Do as he wishes, please, for my sake.'

There was an inquest on the dead student. Julian attended. Alana was not required; he had seen to that. A verdict of suicide whilst under the influence of illegal substances—a quantity of heroin had been found amongst his possessions, Julian had seen to that too—was brought in and the matter closed. A few weeks later, however, as Julian was climbing into his car outside the local village bank, a small ferocious-looking woman approached him and accused him of being a murderer. He vaguely remembered her from the inquest. It was the boy's mother, Mrs Keys. After a few more hostile words blurted out of her twisted, tearful face she scurried away and left an embarrassed and angry Julian the object of several strange and unwelcome glances from bystanders.

By the time Alana was sixteen she looked older than her years and had, as Maurice had predicted, become quite a beauty. Julian detected her mother's high cheekbones and slanting eyes which gave her a very alluring and slightly feral look. She moved in a feline way, too. Her intellectual progress had been staggering.

Academically ahead of others her age, several languages mastered, an accomplished musician and sportswoman.

It was around this time that Maurice made another visit. Julian was working in the laboratory late one night when he heard, despite the windstorm outside, a car pull up on the gravel drive.

'You usually let me know,' said an unsettled Julian.

'Yes, I'm sorry,' replied an even more flustered Maurice. 'I had to see you, Julian.'

When the Shadow Minister for Education addressed him by

his first name Julian knew it must be serious. 'I've come straight from the airport, on my way back from a conference in San Francisco.' Julian took him into the study and poured him a glass of whisky.

'What's on your mind, Maurice?'

He was tense, sweating, sitting on the edge of his chair as if it was on fire. 'The project. Our project...'

Julian feared the worst, saw his pioneering work, not to mention the funding, go out of the window. In fact, his work had been very fruitful of late.

'Well, I don't know how far along you are in your work, but...'

'No questions were to be asked about my methods or results,' Julian reminded him imperiously.

'Yes, I know, but... things have changed.' He struggled for words. Julian poured himself a large whisky to steel himself against what seemed to be inevitable disappointment.

'Our people... and it's a very small circle... are preparing for the future, Julian. It's a future of difficult decisions and harsh realities...'

'Stop talking like a bloody politician on the television, Maurice and get to the point.'

Maurice stood up. He had never acknowledged the oil painting on the wall before but now it gained his attention and he stared at it for a few moments.

'The Alchemist,' he muttered to himself before turning to face Julian.

'You'll have to speed up your program Julian. Results. Solid, practical results are what is needed now.'

'Who sent you, Maurice?'

The Minister ignored Julian's question. 'Even you, Julian,

living here in this rustic backwater, must have heard of this new virus that's coming out of the Far East?'

Julian had indeed been keeping up to date with developments. Word of the virus had leaked out amongst the scientific community nine months ago and he had contacted a fellow researcher in China who had told him of its devastating effects. Through various nefarious means he had obtained a sample of the organism and after separating out the serum from the plasma had been injecting black rats and a rare species of bat. The results were alarming. A blood type containing antigens that attacked themselves. For a moment Julian was convinced he had created a new microorganism. He pressed on with his experiments.

'The NHS and other public organisations may very well be overrun,' Maurice continued, his voice becoming more and more strangulated. 'The private sector's time has come. The welfare state, not just here in England but all over the western world won't be able to cope. Something has got to take its place; the public have to be placated... until they can be re-educated that is.'

'Now you sound like a bloody preacher. 'A second coming...'' Julian laughed.

'That's what it is, Julian. That's how they talk, how they think. The wealth of these people is already unimaginable and it's going to increase.'

'Where does science come into this... new order?'

Maurice leaned forward in the chair, screwed his hands together as if in prayer. 'For years now the Americans have had federal laws that permitted tests and trials on certain members of the population... But the liberals, the do-gooders, have made it almost impossible for the program to function effectively.'

Julian knew where this conversation was headed. 'Go on...' he said.

'The racially inferior, the weak and feeble-minded, are holding back progress. People are living to ages that are a drain on resources that could be better used for the fit and healthy.' He stood up and faced Julian squarely. 'I've been asked... instructed...'

He looks like a schoolboy bringing home difficult homework, thought Julian. '...To start up the program over here. You may have been consigned to oblivion in England but your reputation, across the pond, is still considerable, Julian.'

A silence fell on the room. Maurice sat down and settled back into the chair. Julian refilled his glass. 'Who... or what is Bracho?' The question clearly had an effect on his visitor, but Maurice was too skilled an operator to be caught out.

'Three quarters of a million... every six months... conditions the same...' It was at this moment that there was a faint knock on the door and Alana entered.

'Oh, father. I saw a light under the door. I didn't know you had a visitor. I'll speak to you in the morning.'

'Come in, Alana,' Julian insisted. He thought it high time that the Minister should once again confront his, Julian's, most successful experiment.

She stepped into the study but left her hand on the doorknob. Maurice stood up. He was awestruck. Was this the same girl he had witnessed playing the piano all those years ago?

'You remember Maurice Bond.'

'Hello, Mister Bond.' She was fully aware of the effect she had on him but smiled demurely and held out her hand.

'What is it you want, Alana?' asked Julian.

She hesitated.

Julian spoke out. 'It's all right to speak in front of Mister Bond. We have no secrets here.'

'Father. I've decided that I should like to go to university to continue my studies.'

Julian had been expecting this for some time. She was so advanced, had taken, and passed, all the exams required for entry. But he was reluctant to let her go out into the world of people, of men, even though he knew it was inevitable.

'How old are you, Alana?' asked Maurice. He hadn't taken his eyes off her since she appeared.

'Sixteen,' she replied.

'Sixteen! What will you study?'

'Human Sciences.'

'A very worthy subject.'

She turned and addressed Julian. 'I thought of attending your old college.'

'Perhaps we should discuss this further in the morning, Alana.'

'As you wish.' She left the room. Maurice, mouth open, watched the door close behind her and continued to gaze at the space she left behind. Julian waited for a moment, wondering whether Maurice had perceived anything out of the ordinary regarding Alana.

'Your daughter is remarkably assured for her age,' was all he managed to say.

'Three-quarters of a million, I think you said?'

'Er, yes, that's right.' Maurice came back down to earth.

'I will have to engage an assistant. If you want 'results' quickly.'

'Whatever it takes, Julian.' He opened the door. 'My visits may become more frequent from now on.'

'Is that to check up on your investment?'

Maurice was offended. 'Of course. Why else would I...?' Flustered, he left. Julian heard the car on the gravel and the gate close. He took down from the bookshelf his Hermeticum Praxis and began to turn the pages as if reconnecting his own state of mind with that of the ancients. It was his way of recharging his batteries, of convincing himself that the path he had been led down by Professor Meinegen was the only way. He turned his attention to the Alchemist in the painting and marvelled at the timeless nature of his existence, as relevant then as it was now. As he stared at every detail he was reminded of the shadowy figure of the Alchemist's assistant in the background and his thoughts turned to the dilemma of finding his own 'assistant'. Who could he trust? He knew the answer before he had asked himself the question... but how to find him?

Chapter 12

Thomas Alfred Creighton stood behind the counter polishing a glass. He was watching the small colour television that occupied a shelf over the dartboard. Through the open door came the lapping sound of the sea and the distant hum of traffic from the autopista. He hadn't noticeably aged in his time spent away from England and still maintained that slightly unkempt student look. A couple of elderly men were playing cards at a table in the corner. At this time of day, most of the locals were taking their siesta.

Creighton idly had one eye on a news item from the BBC—he liked to keep in touch with events from 'home'—when a familiar face appeared. It was Maurice Bond. Creighton remembered him as one of his erstwhile employers, Professor Julian Hawkes, associates. The ubiquitous politician was getting married at a picturesque setting by the lake of Lucerne. A small gathering of family and guests and amongst them, looking a deal older and none too happy, was Julian. Creighton's surprise was further fuelled by the bride. She was much younger than the groom, beautiful in an otherworldly way and seemingly indifferent to the fuss surrounding the event. His mouth open in astonishment he put down the glass. 'Could it be…? Surely not…!' He did the sums in his head. 'It was nineteen years since…' Then the penny dropped…

The broadcast ended as abruptly as it had started and returned to the studio and the sports news. Creighton was aghast as the memories came flooding back. His face turned pale, and he had to steady himself against the bar. After Julian's ultimatum and after he had carried out the final task assigned to him... well, partially...

Creighton had decamped to Spain where he looked up an old school friend. A drop-out like himself, the friend had reluctantly agreed to let him stay for a few days. When he found out that Creighton had money, he became less hostile and invited him to, not only extend his visit, but to invest in the tapas bar he owned a few miles down the coast from Malaga. The friend, Jack Bellingham, had been rusticated from Cambridge for stealing from a charity fund set up to help famine victims in Africa. Creighton applauded the decision reached by the University Board but secretly he admired the nerve displayed by Jack—it was the beginning of his own rebellion.

A few weeks after a deal was struck between the two 'partners in crime', the leaking roof was fixed, a new set of tables and chairs was installed and a sign, 'El Perro Muerto', hung over the door. Jack didn't care for the new name, but Creighton insisted. 'It has sentimental associations,' he explained.

Creighton hadn't let on to his new business partner about the existence of Alice. A few days after the bar opened, he flew back to England via Dublin and returned to Spain with Alice a few days later. Creighton explained to Jack that she was a distant relative with a long-term illness and had to be kept on a permanent diet of medication which accounted for her odd behaviour. Alice settled into the upstairs bedroom and, much to Jack's annoyance, gradually transferred the contempt she held for Creighton to include him as well.

Creighton hadn't complied with his 'master's' order to do away with her. He had quickly realised that one day, she might be of some use, although he hadn't worked out quite how useful. The threesome rubbed along for a time until, conveniently, Jack was run over and killed by a coach carrying a party of Chinese tourists to the airport and so the cafe became the property of Creighton. The locals assumed that Alice was his wife, but no such arrangement had been made. She was as much a burden to Creighton as she was a companion in bed.

Their relationship had inevitably become physical out of a mutual need rather than out of any affection. They tolerated each other. He ran the cafe, did the shopping, prepared the tapas, and served the drinks. Alice rarely ventured outside and was only occasionally seen behind the bar, a situation which most of the elderly patrons regarded as correct. But Creighton knew that one day the past would rein in the present and his decision to spare her life would pay off.

The news report of the wedding in Switzerland and the sight of Julian had set his mind racing. He contemplated a sweet revenge but knew that he would have to box clever. After all, the esteemed scientist knew where the body was buried.

One of the card players, an old man wearing a black beret, approached the counter and put down a few coins. He gave Creighton a queer look. 'Que pasa?' Creighton took a moment to respond. 'De nada… nada', and he took the payment and watched the old man join his friend outside the cafe. He walked round the bar, crossed the floor, and closed the door, there wouldn't be any other customers until the heat abated and the evening cool came down. Lately he had become mindful of the parlous state of the cafe's finances. He had spent a bit improving the place—the television which illegally showed football matches, lino tiles on the floor, a wi-fi connection—but they hadn't made much difference. The locals were people of habit, and he noticed the same old faces in front of him day after day. In one of her few sober moods Alice had advised him to invest.

There was a plot of empty land adjacent to the building which ran down to the beach. 'Extend the back of the cafe and open a restaurant that looks out over the sea,' she urged him. But he wasn't really interested. 'No ambition that's your trouble,' she taunted him and poured herself a large gin. But she was right. As long as everything ticked over, he was... well, not happy, but prepared to bide his time. And now, it seemed, the time had come.

Carefully, methodically, as he lay in bed that night, he formulated a plan and in the early hours of the morning he crept downstairs and, standing behind the bar, wrote a letter. *'Dear Professor Hawkes, could an old associate of yours remind you of the close bond that ties us together...'* He considered the use of the word 'bond' a clever touch knowing that it would strike a chord with his erstwhile employer. The next morning, he walked along the dusty main road to the 'Oficina de Correos' and posted the letter.

'You were up early,' came Alice's carping comment from amongst the bedclothes on his return.

'I decided to act on your advice, my sweet, and make an investment', he replied.

She sat up. 'In what?'

'The future. What else?'

Chapter 13

Since Maurice's appearance on that fated stormy night, events had moved rapidly. Alana had indeed gone to university. Against all of Julian's advice, objections, and eventual pleading, her strong will had prevailed. One balmy September morning she said goodbye to her infirm mother. Joan was suitably tearful, but Alana maintained an unruffled demeanour. 'I'll come back in the holidays, mother.'

The night before her departure, Joan had explained to Alana that she was adopted, that she and Julian were not her biological parents. She hadn't told Julian of her decision to inform their daughter, but she felt that Alana should know before going out into the world. Alana accepted the news with an indifference that was chilling. 'I thought as much, mother. I'm not a bit like you or father.' Joan managed to regain her faculties and said, 'perhaps it would be best not to tell your father that I told you…'

Julian, reluctantly, drove her to Cambridge. Nothing was said during the journey.

The student who helped bring up Alana's luggage lingered in the doorway of her room, staring at her, until Julian closed the door on him. 'You see how it will be?'

She had ignored them both, fully aware of the affect she had on men and boys. 'But this is your old college. If it was good enough for you.'

'You don't need it, you're brighter than all the other clods put together, I've seen to that.'

'And I'm grateful, father... or should I refer to you as my stepfather because that's who you are.' Julian was stunned. How did she...? Who could have...? Joan. It must have been her!

A knock at the door interrupted their exchange and Dean Frost entered. He was a thin, elderly man, wearing cap and gown. He shook Julian's hand. 'Professor Hawkes... welcome back.' It was if all past disputes had been forgotten. 'And this must be Alana.' They too shook hands. 'I just wanted to welcome you and make sure you are settling in happily.'

'Yes, thank you,' replied Alana.

'Good. Good. It's an honour for our college to receive the offspring of one of its most eminent alumni.'

'Don't you mean notorious?' said Julian in a deliberately abrasive manner.

The Dean laughed awkwardly. 'But we don't recognise any sort of favouritism here. You'll have to stand on your own two feet, young lady.'

'That's exactly what I intend to do.' Her assured tone startled the Dean who retreated towards the door. 'Well, I'll leave you to unpack,' and he closed the door behind him.

Julian regarded Alana with a mixture of pride and apprehension. She was his creation. Up to this moment he had moulded her, guided her, but now she was embarking on her own path, becoming something—someone—he thought that, in the future, he may not recognise.

'I'll be leaving as well,' said Julian.

'As you wish, Julian,' came her reply as she opened her suitcase.

'Alana, if anything...'

She cut him off abruptly. 'Goodbye. I don't expect we'll see each other for some time.'

Julian was shocked by her callous delivery but managed to control himself. Unable to think of anything further to say he turned and left the room. In the car, as he drove home, he reflected on his handiwork. For the first time he was faced with the possibility that his creation was not as perfect as he believed her to be. Perhaps, being with others her own age would change her, would give her some 'heart'…he couldn't think of a better word to describe her indifference to others.

He decided not to take Joan to task about the adoption issue. What difference does it make now, he convinced himself.

'Will she be all right?' asked Joan. 'She seemed so… well, not at all upset about going. Did she say anything in the car?'

'Oh, she'll be fine. It wouldn't surprise me if in six months' time she was running the place,' came his testy reply. She was too weak to take issue with him and lay back on her pillow. Their relationship had deteriorated over time. He still brought her meals up to her, but the days of asking for advice from his once trusted lab assistant were over.

He repaired to the laboratory, the only place he felt safe and secure. As he entered, he noticed that even the Mother Plant in its glass chamber seemed to have wilted. He had been experimenting with the mandragora leaves that he had frozen all those years ago, looking for abnormal cells that could be grafted onto healthy ones. Much to his frustration things had not been going well. He knew he needed fresh organisms to play with.

Maurice was a frequent visitor, eager to know how the 'program' was coming along. As long as Alana was at home Julian knew he could fob him off with scientific blather. He was horrified by the politician's more than casual interest in her progress. Maurice had offered to introduce Alana into the ever-expanding world of AI technology, an area that Julian regarded with some suspicion.

'Nonsense. It's nothing to be frightened of and, Julian, you'd better get up to speed. It's going to change our way of doing things.' Partly as a way of keeping an eye on them Julian agreed to sit in on the computer sessions and, after a while, he realised the potential. It wasn't long before he had persuaded Maurice to invest in a whole new digital laboratory.

The first incident came a few months after Alana had left home for university. There had been no word, no letter, no phone call, no text message, no e-mail to indicate how she was getting on. When Julian received the phone call from her college, he had just closed the front door on the doctor who had paid a call on Joan whose influenza had taken a turn for the worst. 'Your wife should be in hospital Mister Hawkes,' he repeated.

'You know as well as I do that if she goes into hospital she won't ever come out.'

That's as maybe,' he commented rather bleakly handing Julian a prescription for antibiotics.

Julian picked up the receiver.

'Professor Hawkes?'

'Speaking.'

'It's Dean Frost here. I think you should come at once.'

Julian jumped into his car and sped off towards Cambridge. The Dean had assured him that Alana was all right but vague about what the trouble was. When he arrived, an ambulance was parked at the entrance to chambers. A crowd of students were gathered round, kept at a safe distance by a couple of uniformed policemen. Two medics carried out a gurney on which was a body covered by a sheet. Dean Frost, a grave expression on his face, led Julian up to his study in the main building. Alana was sitting with her back to the window, an open book on her lap, seemingly ignorant of events below. Julian was introduced to her philosophy tutor, who was clearly upset and a rather young-looking detective. Dean Frost then dismissed the tutor who gratefully scurried away.

'What about my tutorial?' asked Alana. Julian went and sat with his daughter. The detective explained that one of the students, James Blake, had hanged himself on the landing area just outside her room.

'Did you know him, Alana?' Julian inquired.

'He was in my philosophy class,' came her matter-of-fact reply.

The sound of the ambulance driving away came up from the quadrangle below.

'I've managed to find out from questioning a few of the other students that this James Blake had a… crush, on your daughter,' said the detective.

'Are you suggesting that she had anything to do with this business?' Julian responded angrily.

'I'm not suggesting anything, sir. Just appraising you of the facts as we know them.'

'Now, now, gentlemen,' interrupted Dean Frost. 'This is not the time or place for accusations or recriminations.'

After a few more questions the detective left. Dean Frost also made as if to leave. 'I must attend to certain matters, Professor Hawkes. The boy's parents are flying in from Portugal.' He hesitated in the doorway. 'Oh dear, what a terrible business.'

Julian was glad they were alone. He was mindful of the piano teacher who had dispatched himself in a similar manner.

'Alana, what can you tell me that you haven't already told the police?'

'Nothing.'

'Was this young man sweet on you?'

'Don't treat me like a child, Julian. He was just one of the boys in the same class as me. I cannot be responsible for what goes on in their immature minds.'

What she didn't tell Julian was that the previous night she and three of her fellow male students, amongst them James Blake, were engaged in a drinking session that had got out of control. Lolling on chairs and on the floor, in various stages of undress, glasses and bottles in hand, marijuana smoke filling the air, the four young men watched as Alana, the only one not in a state of intoxication, performed a striptease. She disrobed in a cool and calculating manner, eyeballing each of the young men in turn. When one of them staggered too close to her and lit up a 'joint', she was momentarily alarmed by the flame from the lighter, grabbed a glass of vodka and put it out. The others laughed. At the exact moment she removed the final garment, James Blake, got uneasily to his feet and pushed and shoved the other two complaining students out of the room. As he turned to face Alana, he was surprised to see that she had disappeared. But a light from the bedroom and a moving shadow caused him to grin expectantly. He took a swig from a wine bottle. As he advanced towards the bedroom, a lascivious gleam in his eye, Alana appeared, fully dressed.

'What?' his befuddled voice blurted out.

'The game's over.'

'Game?' He teetered and had to hold on to a chair back. 'This isn't a fucking game.' He made a lunge for her, but she pushed him away with some ease. He stumbled and sank to his knees.

'Maybe... when you've grown up.'

'Fucking prick teaser...!' he yelled at her. Frustrated and

angry, the hapless young man tried to get to his feet but began to choke on his own spittle. As he dashed for the bathroom, he was violently sick. He ran the tap and splashed cold water over his face. He looked in the mirror. Alana, in the hallway, regarded him with cold indifference before closing the front door quietly behind her.

For Alana it had been a kind of experiment. Aware of the social aspect of student life, conscious of the effect she had on her fellows, even some of the female students had expressed interest, she had decided to carry out a test of the lengths they were prepared to go. But she quickly tired of the experiment and returned to her room. She had heard, in the early hours of the morning, a light tapping on her door and the ensuing scrabble of feet but had ignored the sounds and gone back to sleep.

Nothing came of the affair. A verdict of suicide was pronounced on the boy and his unhappy parents returned to their retirement villa in Portugal.

When, a few weeks later, Joan died of pneumonia, Julian contacted Alana by letter and offered to come and fetch her home. 'I realise she wasn't your birth mother, but she loved you just the same…' She didn't respond. Julian wondered, for a moment, what sort of creature he had created.

He and a very old and frail Mrs Craddock were the only ones at her cremation. A lay preacher said a few consoling words and it was all over. Maurice arrived at the crematorium as they were leaving. He climbed out of the chauffeur driven ministerial car. 'I'm sorry, Julian.' Julian nodded his head by way of a reply.

Maurice looked around anxiously. 'Where's…?'

Julian wondered whether he should, at last, tell Maurice about the 'successes' of his work on genetics but decided against it. There would be a better time and place. He returned to the empty 'Mendes House', climbed the stairs to Joan's bedroom, closed the door and locked it. The key he placed at the back of a drawer in his study. The following day he called a local firm who specialised in house clearances and told them he required a room clearance only. The next day a large white van turned up. Supervised closely by Julian, a man and a teenage boy were admitted to Joan's bedroom where they took everything away. He paid them in cash and watched as the last vestiges of his wife were driven away.

A year passed which Julian spent hard at work in the laboratory. The introduction of the latest digital equipment made his task a lot easier, but he was still hampered by a lack of living cells on which to practice. He was reticent about broaching the matter with Maurice because he was unsure how far, ethically, he could go. Perhaps, he reflected, it was advancing years that caused his reservations, after all 'ethical considerations' had never held him hostage before.

Late in February Julian attended a conference at Westminster Hall. He hated travelling up to London—the crowds, and the noise—but Maurice had insisted that he come. It was less a conference, more a public relations exercise with various private companies touting for business. The banner over the entrance read, 'A New Partnership for the NHS'. Julian wasn't fooled for a minute. Maurice, looking very pleased with himself, was fronting a kiosk bearing the logo, 'The Bracho Institute - Health for All'. Maurice introduced Julian to his shiny-suited partner, 35-year-old Jack Goode, and the representative from the NHS, Jane Robinson, a rather dowdy-looking woman with a pronounced lisp.

'The great Professor Julian Hawkes, welcome,' announced Jack, and he shook Julian's hand with great vigour and followed up with a slap on the back as if they had known each other for years. 'Maurice has told me all about you.' His arrogant manner and the way he waved his mobile phone around as if it was a conductor's baton, immediately rubbed Julian up the wrong way. Jane Robinson nodded a more reserved greeting. Julian had a feeling that his notoriety had preceded him and that she didn't quite approve. After introductions were over and a weak cup of coffee had been provided by an attractive young female intern named Chloe, Julian took Maurice aside. 'Why am I here, Maurice?'

'To add scientific gravitas,' came his reply. 'And there's someone I want you to meet.'

Julian looked around the hall, already bustling with what looked like salesman and hustlers of the worst kind. Jack Goode was prominent amongst them, shaking hands and slapping backs.

'Who?' Asked Julian.

'At around midday…'

And sure enough, just after noon there was a flurry of activity near the entrance of the hall and a pack of newspapermen, photographers and television reporters entered. Amongst them was a group of security men and nestled amongst them was the Prime Minister, grinning as if his life depended on it, waving to some, shaking the hands of others, skilfully avoiding the barrage of questions regarding the latest political scandal aimed his way by the press. The entourage, now led by dynamic Jack, his mobile defining their route, made straight for the kiosk and the security guards sealed off the area from the paparazzi. The PM greeted Maurice like an old friend. His introduction to Julian was a little more formal. 'Professor Hawkins, at last. Your work for us is indispensable.'

He swept on, meeting and greeting, and as suddenly as the

throng had arrived it moved on to another part of the hall. The mispronunciation of his surname hadn't pleased Julian but, he thought, he had referred to 'us'.

The intrigue went all the way to the top. 'Well, what do you think?' said Maurice.

'Does he never stop grinning?'

'Great, isn't it? From now on there are no limits. You can see that.'

'Is that the only reason you asked me here?' asked a rather irritated Julian.

Maurice blushed. 'Not entirely.' Julian was suddenly aware of someone standing just behind him. He turned and beheld a very smart, sophisticated Alana, standing there. She was dressed in a very expensive tailored suit; her hair was neatly piled up on her head and she wore designer sunglasses. 'Hello,' and she proffered a hand. Julian, startled, took it. He had heard, from a roundabout route, that she had left University after taking, and passing, all her exams and was now working for an independent 'think-tank' somewhere in the city. Alana let go of Julian's hand, moved to the side of Maurice, and took his arm. Now, Julian was shocked… and speechless.

'You mentioned something about lunch, Maurice.'

'So I did. Care to join us, Julian?'

Julian managed to gather himself together. 'Er, no. Thanks all the same. Nice to see you again, Alana…' He watched them stroll away, arm in arm, across the busy hall.

'Going to stay for tonight's beano, Professor?' inquired Jack, his brash delivery staying Julian's befuddled thoughts. Before Julian could answer and without waiting for a reply, Jack clamped his mobile to his ear and took a call. Julian shook his head and strode away. He had lost her, his creation, to someone almost twice her age.

As he sat on the train taking him home, he wondered whether now was the time to own up that Alana was not as other mortals, that her provenance could be viewed as, at best controversial, at worst dubious. Three months later the wedding invitation arrived together with an airplane ticket, hotel reservation and travel itinerary. Nothing from Alana, just a note scrawled by Maurice, *'See you by the lake.'*

It was when Julian returned to the 'Mendes House' that he found a letter, postmarked from Spain, in the letter box.

Chapter 14

Creighton turned up late one night, alone and soaked through. The taxi driver, a grumpy Pole, had been unable to find the address and, after an argument over the fare, Creighton had walked the last few miles in the pouring rain.

Julian was working in the laboratory when the doorbell rang. He had spent the best part of the day studying the effects of different soil compounds on the mandragora cuttings. Two specimens had been in the incubator overnight. One cutting was growing in an organically prepared soil, the other in a portion of the 'dead soil' that had spawned the Mother Plant from the Davos greenhouse. The first specimen had wilted, the leaf was brown, dying. By way of contrast the graft planted in the 'dead soil' was vibrant, green, flourishing. Julian was not surprised at the outcome. He threw the dead plant into a bin and placed the thriving one into the chamber with the Mother Plant. Immediately he noticed a quiver of movement. He was about to remove the cutting to see if the activity died down when he heard the distant sound of the front doorbell.

He was startled by the figure standing in the porch, suitcase in hand. 'Good evening, Professor,' came the sardonic greeting.

Julian had replied to Creighton's letter and expected a reply in turn, but none had come and so he was considering whether to write again, this time with a firm offer. Creighton, for his part, had been surprised by Julian's reply, inviting him, in a begrudgingly vague way, to return and take up his post as assistant. There were no indications as to what kind of work the Professor was engaged in, but Creighton had no illusions as to their no doubt disreputable nature.

He stepped in out of the rain and put down the suitcase, his drenched clothes dripping on to the floor. They eyed each other with mutual suspicion.

'You'd better get out of those wet things. Don't want you sick and unable to work.' Julian showed him upstairs, to a small room under the roof at the far end of the house, and left him with a brusque, 'you can sleep here for tonight.'

Creighton was somewhat relieved that there had been no row, no recriminations, no accusations, but he knew that no doubt they would surface later.

Having made up his mind to return to England, Creighton had explained to Alice that he had been offered a job of work more lucrative than the tapas bar provided and that he would send for her as soon as he was settled. In her addled state she didn't really understand and kicked up a fuss, but he managed to calm her by promising that, while he was back in England, he would see if he could track down her child that had been put up for adoption. This hollow pledge reduced Alice to tears of gratitude. They had never talked of her traumatic time all those years ago but now that it was out in the open, he was able to threaten her with, 'but the deal only works if you stay off the sauce and keep on taking your pills.' He knew that her drinking would continue unabated but that she was sometimes forgetful with her medication. It was important, for his grand plan, that she remain confused and dependent.

He got out of his wet clothes, put on his pajamas, climbed into the single bed, and turned out the light. As he lay there, the rain hammering down on the roof just over his head, he congratulated himself on his unscrupulous scheming. He was 'back in the fold', the outcast restored.

Julian tried to work on for a time on his cuttings before retiring but he had been disturbed by his erstwhile assistant's sudden, unannounced appearance. It was as if Creighton had planned to force the issue and turn up without warning in the hope that he, Julian, had not changed his mind and wouldn't, or couldn't, slam the door in his face. As he mounted the stairs an hour later, he noticed that the light under the door of the spare room was out. He too had a plan. Creighton was not only beholden to him but was bound by murder. Julian knew that he couldn't trust his old assistant but was prepared to let him resume his old position for as long as he, Julian, needed him and then he would make good on his threat to kill him if he ever came back into his life.

Before he went to sleep, he locked the bedroom door and, as a further precaution, took from a drawer in his wardrobe the revolver he had bought on the black market and placed it under his pillow.

The next morning Julian was at work in the lab when Creighton entered. Julian had earlier decided to go on the offensive and let him know exactly where he stood. 'I told you what would happen if you ever came back, Creighton.'

'I considered that and thought it worth the risk.'

'You've spent all the money, then?

'A long time ago.'

'On drugs, no doubt.'

Creighton, too, had planned his response to what, he knew, was going to be an aggressive first exchange.

'That's all behind me, Professor. I'm clean. Got responsibilities now.'

For a moment Julian was alarmed. What did he mean,

'responsibilities?' 'What about Alice? You took care of her?'

'Oh, yes. She was taken care of.'

Julian inwardly relaxed, but still he was on his guard.

Creighton looked around at the brand-new facilities. 'Nice. Must have cost a few quid? Back into research?

Julian leaned back against the bench and folded his arms. He was keen to know what Creighton really wanted, why he had turned up so readily. He watched the pale, skinny ex-student as he walked around the lab, inspecting the equipment. He stopped at the chamber and peered in at the Mandragora. 'Our old friend,' he said in a sneering way. The Mother Plant shivered. 'Must be quite difficult for you, all alone in this big house. Especially now with your wife gone and your stepdaughter moving in such high-flying circles.'

Julian bristled. Of course, Creighton had seen or read about the wedding and, after putting two and two together had written the begging letter. 'Get to the point, Creighton. What is worth risking your life for? Money... a job?'

'Actually, both of those. But the circumstances would have to be different.'

'How different.'

Creighton considered the surroundings, the whiteness, the cleanliness, a long way from the shabby workings of a loss-making cafe on the coast of Spain. 'Well, I could be very comfortable here, close to work, very cosy. Just the two of us.'

Julian decided, as a conciliatory act, to offer an olive branch. He knew from past experience Creighton's weaknesses; how receptive to a bribe he was. 'I have to admit there have been occasions when I could've done with some assistance.'

'I knew you'd see it my way. I'd need paying, regularly... and weekends off, of course,' he blurted out impetuously.

'Of course,' replied Julian. He approached Creighton and grabbed hold of his jacket lapel. 'But a word of warning. At any time, my daughter may return home. If you so much as make any contact with her I will have no compunction in killing you... this time.'

Creighton was suddenly reminded of how dangerous his 'Master' could be. And he didn't have to wait long before his assumption that 'work' in the lab was going to be a continuation of previous assignments was proved correct.

Julian had given him a 'crash course' on his experiments up until now and was pleasantly surprised that Creighton had retained much of the knowledge and working practices that he had instilled in him.

One day, after Julian had left the house for a meeting in London, Creighton was cleaning up in the laboratory and he paused for a moment in front of the Mother Plant. He still regarded the plant with a possessiveness that bordered on obsession. 'After all,' he reflected, 'I was there at your birth, and it was I who cared for you...' He lifted the glass front of the chamber and reached out to touch one of the tendrils. The plant shrunk back, as if sensing a hostile presence. Angry, Creighton swore and stormed out. In the garden, a few minutes later, as he was burning rubbish in the incinerator, he remembered that he had left the chamber door open, and he returned to find the Mandragora shuffling its way out of its glass prison and along the bench top. Horrified, Creighton rushed over and, after an awkward struggle, had managed to get the aberrant plant back inside the chamber. He slammed down the glass and, sweating and gasping, rocked back with relief. It had been like wrestling with a human and he recalled its 'father', Archibald Brasher-

Courtney, attempting to release himself   from his noose. Hurriedly and thoroughly, Creighton cleaned up the mess left after the attempted escape; he   knew what the consequences would be if Julian were to find out about the incident.

As he consigned the few leaves and stems from the Mother Plant that had broken off during the melee to the flames of the incinerator, a few thousand miles away, Alana reacted. She was accompanying her husband on one of His Foreign Office junkets when she had suddenly felt nauseous – her Mother beginning to move – then feint – the struggle – and then she collapsed – the burning. A week in hospital followed, the doctors at a loss to find anything wrong with her.

Three months had gone by when Julian, working alone in the lab, heard a car door slam outside. 'That'll be Creighton,' he told himself and he returned to work. A few minutes later, behind him, the inner door opened.

'Is that you, Creighton?'

No reply was forthcoming and so he looked up to see Alana standing there. She had a travelling bag with her, and she wore a tired, blank expression. There was an awkward, but not unusual, silence between them. Julian had not seen her since the wedding in Switzerland and, although he had 'given her away' at the ceremony, their relationship had not changed in any way.

'Who is Creighton?' she asked innocently.

'My new assistant. He's out running an errand for me. I was expecting him back…'

'I thought I'd spend the weekend here if that's all right?' She seemed, to Julian, unusually tense. 'Where's your husband?'

'Los Angeles…' She glanced at her watch, '… by now.'

Julian knew from her tone that all was not well. 'You usually accompany him on his business trips.'

She shrugged. 'Do I?'

'It may surprise you to know, Alana, that, as your father...'

'Stepfather,' she broke in.

He continued, 'I take a keen interest in your... well-being and...'

She had wandered over to the chamber containing the Mother Plant. As she gazed at it, its leaves began to ripple, the stems to sway, as if aroused by some external force. Alana, in turn, seemed to be intoxicated with the movement inside the chamber. Julian was astonished, but also alarmed by the reaction. He quickly attempted to get her attention. 'By the way of him, Maurice that is, I shouldn't be at all surprised if he isn't leading the Party soon and then? Who knows?'

She turned towards the door. 'Yes, who knows...' she said with a degree of unconcern and left the lab. The mandragora became still again.

After a moment's reflection, Julian returned to the job in hand He took a leaf of the Mandrake plant and cut it with his scalpel...

At the same time, Alana, carrying her overnight bag up the stairs, suddenly faltered, dropped the bag, grabbed the banister with one hand and clutched her neck with the other as a spasm of pain coursed through her body.

Julian heard the thump of her bag rolling down the steps, dropped his scalpel and rushed out into the hallway. 'Are you all right?'

Alana, having regained her balance and indifferent to the workings of her body, nodded her head. 'I'm fine, thank you.'

Julian retrieved her bag and took it up to her. 'Your bedroom is as you left it.'

'Thank you,' and she continued on her way.

He heard the door open and close and, his mind racing with troublesome thoughts, returned to work.

Alana was asleep, fully clothed, on the bed when the sound of a car drawing up outside woke her. She got up, went to the window, and pulled aside the curtain. It was dark outside. A van had parked next to her Audi Coupe and a man was struggling with a smallish bundle wrapped in a blanket. After slinging the bundle over his shoulder, he closed the rear doors, carried it to the side door of the laboratory and entered. 'That must be Julian's assistant,' mused Alana. Puzzled, she let the curtain drop, turned away and started to undress.

Creighton laid the bundle down on a clear surface and watched by an excited looking Julian, pulled back the blanket to reveal the unconscious, but still alive, body of a child.

'How recent?' asked Julian.

'An hour, maybe a bit less.'

Julian picked up the scalpel, hesitated, then held it out to Creighton. 'I trust your anatomical training at University has not deserted you?'

Creighton was surprised. It was the first time his 'Master' had entrusted him with any task other than a menial one. 'It'll be my pleasure…' He began to undress the small boy, firstly taking off his dirty and torn shirt and shorts, then his socks and shoes. Julian dumped the clothes into a waste bin. The boy's breathing was slight but noticeable as they carried the body over to the operating table. Julian put some drops of anaesthetic onto a linen pad and held it over the child's mouth and nose. They waited until the breathing became more regular, then Creighton took up the scalpel and began to slice off sections of tissue from the boy's thigh, depositing them in a petri dish. The first batch Julian placed under the electron microscope for study.

'Perfect,' he exclaimed. 'Now I want you to shave his head and cut some tissue from the parietal lobe.'

Creighton looked up. 'But he's only just alive now?'

'Then hurry…' came back Julian's abrupt command.

Julian had got the idea of using cells from an abnormal source whilst reading a passage from the Hermeticum Praxis. It was a few months before Alana and Creighton had come back into his life. He recalled the words of his old mentor, Professor Josef Meinengen, 'just remember, one must embrace chaos to be able to give birth to a new order.'

With these words turning over in his mind—he was watching the television news the following morning—when a report from Yorkshire caught his attention. Maurice Bond appeared looking very earnest and committed. He was on the campaign trail, electioneering at a school for children with learning difficulties in Leeds. With him was Alana and the odious Jack Goode. A clutch of reporters were also in attendance. They were being shown around the play area of the school by the Chief Administrator of the school, Mrs Kitchin, a middle-aged, middle-class woman wearing sensible clothes, with a no-nonsense attitude who was explaining the cost of caring for a child. Maurice was alert to statistics on the cost and voluble on the future role of government in such institutions. *You hypocrite,* thought Julian. A group of children had gathered round. Some stared directly into the television camera, others moved in a disorderly way around the important visitors. One little girl with Down Syndrome had taken hold of Alana's hand and was gazing up at her. Alana had not withdrawn her hand and at first seemed indifferent to the small child's sweet expression of idolatry.

'Come now, Sally. Leave Mrs Bond alone,' urged Mrs Kitchin, but Sally clung on. Alana looked down at her and in a gesture of mutual affectation crouched down to Sally's level and took both hands in hers. Julian was struck by this apparent spontaneous action and was reminded of the effect Alana had on the Mandragora. Eventually, one of the care assistants came and shepherded the children, including Sally, away. As Alana watched her go, Sally suddenly turned and ran back, burying her face in Alana's dress. After some polite laughter and apologies Sally was ushered back into the schoolhouse. Julian was intrigued and from the following day's newspaper learnt of the school and its location. There was even a picture of the group, including Maurice, Alana and the Down's Syndrome child, Sally Fordham. He formulated a strategy, a possible way of combining cells and mutating them to create a new life form not dissimilar to the way Alana had been created but using deviant cells.

Much to Julian's surprise it had not been difficult persuading Creighton to return to murderous ways. In anticipation of the concessions he knew he would have to make, Julian had had Joan's old bedroom converted to a self-catering apartment with its own back staircase entrance. He gave Creighton the key and showed him the flat the day after he had arrived. He also gave his new assistant a considerable wage, far over and above what he had expected. With the funds from the Bracho Institute regularly arriving in Julian's bank account money was no object. Creighton was stunned by Julian's generosity but was fully aware of the price he would have to pay. And, sure enough, after a few weeks, he received his orders. After finding the location of a Special Needs School not too far away, one dark night with Julian's exhortations ringing in his ears, he had driven out to the site where he had broken into the poorly secured dormitory building and kidnapped a child.

The boy had died very quickly after the first insertion into his brain. Other organs, the heart, liver, and kidneys were extracted and placed in the freezer.

Alana was fast asleep when Creighton carried a slightly lighter bundle out to the van and drove away. Julian was busy preparing samples ready for grafting when Creighton returned. 'I trust you didn't dispose of the body parts in the same place,' he said.

'You forget, I was taught by a master,' replied Creighton in a sardonic way, and he added, 'aren't you going to bed?'

'No time for that. Get me some of the freshest shoots from the greenhouse plants.'

With his new position seemingly secure, Creighton was able to consider the future. He had not forgotten Alice. He wrote to her regularly and received replies, written in her scrawly hand, at a P.O. Box in Cambridge. After a few weeks she threatened to come and join him whether he was ready or not. As he didn't want her impetuosity to spoil his plans he acted quickly and rented a flat in Cambridge, sent her an airplane ticket and some cash and, two days later, met her at the airport. She had obviously not cut down on her drinking, had put on weight and appeared older, blowsier than when he had last seen her in Spain. The tapas bar had been put up for sale and was soon off his hands but there had been some problems getting Alice off the premises and one weekend Creighton had flown down to sort out the mess. 'Why can't I come back with you?' she had begged him. He had stood firm, installed her in a small pension nearby and given her enough money to live comfortably on and made sure she was taking her medication.

'Where the hell have you been?' demanded Julian when Creighton returned a day late and had invented a lame excuse about the van breaking down. Julian, of course, hadn't believed him for a minute. He suspected Creighton of some sort of conspiracy but reminded himself of his usefulness and let the matter go.

Alana came down to breakfast the morning after her return and was sitting in the kitchen drinking a cup of herbal tea when Creighton burst in. He was immediately startled by her presence and, tongue-tied and sleepy after his exertions, he mumbled a 'good morning' and stumbled out. Alana was reminded of the scene she had witnessed during the night but gave it no further thought. She knew that Julian was engaged in important research, Maurice had told her, and she had accompanied him on quite a few of his visits to the Mendes House. Anyway, this morning, she had other things on her mind. She knew that sooner rather than later Maurice would appear and demand to know why she had left him so suddenly in the middle of a very important Foreign Office tour.

Their wedding had featured in 'Hello Magazine' as one of the marriages of the year and the subsequent coverage of their new home in London's Knightsbridge had caused quite a stir. Alana had gone along with all the fuss, realising how important it was for her husband's career. The actual wedding night had been a disaster from Maurice's point of view. She had managed to beat off his physical demands, much to his displeasure. 'Forgive me, Maurice, but I'm just not ready for that,' she said in her matter-of-fact way, which only made him angrier. The truth was that, despite the attributes of her 'parents' she had not come to terms with her sexuality. She had moments of considerable emotion, but they were confused, and she didn't know how to transfer them into physical actions.

She and Maurice eventually came to an arrangement. For

appearances sake she would accompany him on his official visits and tours until… well, that was not specified. She liked Maurice and had done ever since he 'rescued' her from university and gave her a job in a 'think-tank' in the City of London. She was aware of his more than 'fatherly' interest in her, but she had that effect on most men. When one of her fellow workers, a Dane, Edgar, took her out for a meal and then tried to 'touch' her in a taxi, she reacted violently, and he had spent two weeks in hospital after she pushed him out of the moving cab. Maurice once again came to her rescue. He took her away and gave her a job on his own campaign team. When, one day after a weekend in Brighton at the Party Conference, he proposed to her and she said 'yes', it was more out of gratitude than anything else.

Julian, her stepfather, she regarded as her teacher and guardian. There had been no emotional bond between them. At least Maurice respected her and displayed moments of genuine affection. Also, for a time, she appreciated the travel, meeting important people, expensive hotels and meals and Maurice was always buying her gifts. But Alana was aware that there was a discontinuity between the outside world with all its trappings and her inner self. On her seventh birthday she had asked Julian, 'if you are my father, is mummy my real mother?' He had told her that, yes, she was, and left it at that. At University, when one of the students had asked if her father was the infamous Professor Julian Hawkes, she had replied that he was, but why 'infamous' she queried. The story of his radical views and contentious teaching methods came as a surprise to Alana and amongst the information gleaned was the germ of a rumour about her parentage. As she withdrew from Maurice's life and work, she began to contemplate her own beginnings.

It was these thoughts that occupied her as Julian entered the kitchen.

'I see you have met my assistant.'

'Well, not really,' she replied. 'He came in, saw me and bolted.'

Julian, laughed, poured himself a cup of coffee and sat down opposite her. 'You won't have any contact with him. His room is self-contained, and he spends most of his time in the laboratory with me. Should you bump into him while you are here, just ignore him.'

Alana gave him a puzzled look. 'Won't that be rather rude?'

'Please do as I say, Alana.'

There was a moments awkward silence before Julian asked, 'Anyway, how long are you staying?' There came no reply, so he tried again. 'I mean, you are welcome for as long as you like but… when can we expect the Right Honourable Gentleman to turn up?'

Alana frowned and lowered her head. 'I've left him. For good.' The delight on Julian's face was poorly concealed but before he could say anything she said, 'I was adopted, Julian, wasn't I? Joan was not my real mother any more than you are my real father.' There was a hint of disappointment in her voice.

Julian was dumbfounded. 'Why do you ask?'

'I should like to know who my birth parents were.'

Julian hesitated before he lied. 'You were an orphan… parent's unknown.' Then he added hastily, 'It was a condition of the adoption. Your mother, Joan, wanted it that way.'

She looked at him, that blank stare that disconcerted so many.

'I'm sorry, Alana,' was the most he could offer, and he stood up and went off to the lab to begin the day's work.

Alana wasn't convinced. She knew Julian was as devious as he was dishonest.

The cell grafts were, in most cases, thriving. The mutations were providing valuable information for Julian and when Maurice came calling, about a week after Alana had arrived, he was able to show his visitor some startling results.

Julian sensed his anxiety. 'Maurice must know she's here so why doesn't he say anything?' he asked himself. Instead, Maurice listened intently as Julian showed him the results of his tests and the latest experiments he was involved in.

'Will we be able to use this... data for practical purposes?' Maurice asked, a desperate tone in his voice. 'I'm getting pressure from above. They want results, tangible results, not just another list of formulas and data.'

Alana, from her bedroom window, had seen Maurice's car on the drive and wasn't ready to speak with him. She sat on the bed, undecided about what to do. For the first time in her life she felt matters were moving at a pace beyond her control. 'Perhaps I should go down, face him and get it over with', she told herself. And she stood up, smoothed down her dress and left the room.

On the landing, a noise from outside distracted her. She went to the window and looked down into the back garden. Creighton appeared below carrying a large waste bin from the laboratory. He had started a fire in the incinerator and tipped the rubbish in. A dirty, grey smoke soon billowed up and blew across the garden. She watched him as he stood by the incinerator poking at the contents with a bamboo cane. There was something about Julian's assistant that made her uneasy. When he was tending the plants in the greenhouse, she felt a cold shiver down her arms and back which was in contrast to the warmer feeling she received when she was near the Mother Plant. Julian had decreed the hot house 'off limits' to her but one day, when he had driven into town, she had defied him, slid open the door and stepped inside. The plants immediately reacted, their tendrils stretched out towards her, caressed her, enveloped her. The thrill, the feeling of ecstasy was overwhelming. And whenever she was feeling low, and the opportunity presented itself, she would visit her 'friends'.

Another noise, a car door slamming, brought her back to earth. She hoped it was Maurice driving away. She left her room and stood on the landing and, through the net curtain, watched as his car drove away down the lane. Relieved, she went downstairs.

Julian was standing in the hall, an anxious expression on his face. He looked up as Alana descended. 'You're going to have to face him sometime, Alana.'

'I know. But on my terms, not his,' came her reply.

Julian was used to her indifference, even though he found it frustrating because it meant that they could never engage in any meaningful discussion. He frowned and entered his study, another part of the house that was forbidden to Alana. He closed the door behind him, locked it and turned on the television. The news report was in that sensational style so popular with the BBC. '... *the Downs Syndrome boy, Johnny Briggs' whereabouts are still unknown, and his disappearance is causing grave concern. At present the police are not ruling out...*' At first Julian didn't make the connection, then, gradually, he realised what he was watching. He was unmoved. 'Am I becoming like my daughter?' he wondered, 'unable to feel...' He turned off the television, reached for the Hermeticum Praxis and turned to the page that dealt with mutants and their avatars. He studied the ancient text, cast his eyes over the engravings... 'Here is the justification,' he told himself. 'It's all in here. My work must go on...' His eyes gleaming manically, he left the room and, book clutched under his arm, strode towards the laboratory. Creighton had finished emptying the waste bin and was cleaning the equipment used in last night's operation.

'That should have been done directly after…' boomed Julian. 'And what have you done with the clothes?'

'Burning, out there,' replied Creighton, jerking his head in the direction of the garden. Smoke was still surging out of the incinerator, Julian could see it through the window, but before he could say anything Creighton continued, 'Don't worry. I closed the greenhouse door.'

Julian was used to his assistant's surly attitude, but a new tone had entered his manner. There was a defiance, an assurance about him, as if he had a plan. 'Yes,' Julian mused, 'I will have to keep an eye on Thomas Alfred Creighton. A very keen eye…'

Creighton, too, had noticed a change in his employer's demeanour. Yes, he was the same brilliant, opinionated, headstrong scientist, but now an element of desperation had entered his work. Sometimes he wouldn't leave the lab for days at a time, sleeping fitfully on a stool, his head and arms folded on the bench. Creighton began to wonder whether his 'Master' was losing his mind… or was he just human after all?

Chapter 15

Now, with time pressing, with Maurice demanding results, Julian plunged even deeper into his work. The wider implications of what he had done didn't occupy his mind. If he had thought about the kidnappings and murders, he would have reasoned, as he had before, that Creighton was solely responsible. The same parameters applied, who would believe the ravings of a drug addict with a criminal record over the word of a respected Professor of Genetics. Now was his time to prove that in the endless and rather tiresome argument of 'nature versus nurture' his experiments would show the world that both views could be subverted. Alana was living proof that human cells combined with plant cells could produce an ideal synthesis. What was to stop him showing that the same principal would apply to abnormal cells? The medical possibilities were enormous—the prevention of mental and physical abnormalities in the early stages of pregnancy and then, beyond that, the creation of perfect cell types leading to genetic perfection. Designer babies were as desirable as designer clothes he reasoned. And the financial advantages, as Maurice often explained, were huge. 'Just imagine,' he liked to say, 'a tax-free society, all the money you earn is yours to spend as you want.'

One day, not long after Creighton's night drive, Julian heard the, by now, familiar sound of car tyres scrunching on the gravel drive. He knew that it was not his assistant as he had been sent on an errand that would take all day to execute. 'It must be Maurice,' he groaned to himself. The bell rang and Julian opened the front door and was surprised to see, standing there, dressed like a bookie's runner, mobile in hand, the odious Jack Goode. He smiled, thrust out his hand and stepped into the hallway. 'Maurice couldn't come so he sent me'. Julian was indifferent to his visitor.

'Jack Goode, we met at the conference.'

'I remember.' Julian was unsure of how much the young man knew of his brief and the experiments he was conducting. He would have to be careful about what he said and did. 'How can I help you?'

'Nice place,' he said glancing around. 'Got lots of character these old houses.'

'I'm very busy at the moment, so if you could state your business?' pressed Julian.

'Oh, don't let me hold you up, Professor. You just carry on...' His manner was flippant. His eyes strayed up the stairs and instantly Julian knew why he had come. He was looking for Alana. It was possible that Maurice hadn't sent him in his place but that the shallow creature standing before him, full of false bonhomie and dubious intentions, was on a mission of his own making.

Julian was instantly hostile but didn't let his feelings be shown. 'No doubt you would like to see the results of my latest experiments?' Julian said and he led him across the hall and into the laboratory. 'Interested in cell grafting, are you?'

'Actually, my degree is in business studies,' replied Jack.

'Then, perhaps you would like to see a list of expenditures and disbursements? I have all the receipts here...' and he opened a drawer and took out a Manila envelope full of paperwork and dumped it onto the bench. Jack looked baffled. 'Very old-fashioned. I do all my accounting on-line,' he sneered. His attention was then drawn to the Mandragora plant in the observation chamber. With a slightly puzzled look on his face as he asked, 'what is it?'

'Mandragora Officinarum. It's grown for its medicinal qualities... amongst other things.' Julian had decided to play games with the upstart.

Jack shuddered. 'Other things?' he enquirer half-heartedly.

'Go and catch a falling star, Get with child a mandrake root, Tell me where all past years are, Or who cleft the devil's foot.' Julian's dulcet tone, the one he used when lecturing to students and had employed when dispatching Archie Brasher, hung in the air.

Jack wore a baffled expression. Clearly, he surmised, the man before him was deranged.

'It's a poem by John Donne,' explained Julian.

Jack was none the wiser but quickly regained his supercilious manner. 'Actually, I am here for a particular reason, Professor Hawkes.'

At last, thought Julian, *we are getting down to brass tacks.*

'I have a message for Mrs Bond... from her husband.'

Julian turned his back to show his contempt for the messenger. 'Tell me and I will pass it on to my daughter.' There was a long pause, then came the lie. 'But I was told to deliver it personally.'

'If Maurice Bond can trust you, you can trust me.'

Another pause, this time accompanied by an awkward shuffle of feet. 'It's of a confidential nature.'

'It won't leave this room.' Julian had all the answers.

Jack knew when he had come up against a brick wall, but he was smart enough to maintain a stubborn defiance and he said nothing, hoping that the ball would bounce back into Julian's court. Julian let a few minutes pass, his back still firmly positioned in Jack's face, then he turned and opened the door which led into the garden. 'Wait out here.'

Jack, reluctant at first, eventually walked out onto the patio and Julian closed the door behind him.

It was a cold, blustery day. Leaves were blowing everywhere. Jack looked around, at the house, the garden, the empty paddock, and wondered what the Professor was playing at. He wandered over to the greenhouse and was surprised to see the same mandragora plants growing within, dozens of them. He slid back the door and peered inside. The green foliage recoiled from the blast of cold air. He held up his phone and took a picture.

'Shut that door.' Julian strode angrily from the house. With him was Alana. She didn't acknowledge Jack at all.

'Hello, Alana,' he said.

'In Maurice's exact words. We don't want there to be any misunderstandings,' said Julian.

'Please come back to me. I miss you terribly. I will do anything,' Jack relayed in a monotonous tone.

Julian let out a brief laugh of scorn. 'The sort of thing I would expect from a lovesick teenager or in a Mills and Boon novel.' He looked over at Alana. 'What do you think?'

Before she could say anything, Jack butted in. 'If you pack a bag, I could drive you back to London.'

Julian was immediately alarmed and blurted out, 'She has her own car.'

Alana regarded both men with tiresome disdain, turned and went back into the house. She was confused as to what to do. She was aware of social conventions and remembered the vows made at her marriage to Maurice, but it was as if she was being forced into a corner and had to make up new rules from day to day.

From the landing window she saw Jack drive away. She knew of his feelings for her. But he had an eye for any girl who swung into his orbit. She recalled the day of the conference and the party afterwards. She had inadvertently come across Jack and Chloe, the intern, in a sweaty embrace behind the kiosk. Ever since that moment, Jack had been attempting to get close to her, no doubt, she thought, to explain and make amends lest she should tell her husband. How devious, how immature, how trifling their lives were.

She entered her bedroom and shut the door firmly. On the bed was a small, glossy pamphlet. Surprised, she picked it up and read the cover. *'Find Your Birth Parents. The A1 Parenting Agency.'* There was a telephone number and an e-mail address below a series of pictures of happy, smiling children with their happy, smiling parents.

Mystified as to who had left the information for her to see she sat down on the bed. It couldn't have been Julian. The only other person was… Creighton? What game was he playing? She opened the leaflet, examined the contents, and felt a pang of emotion that she had not felt before. Were these children better off than her? She reflected that her upbringing had not been unhappy. She had never wanted for anything. Even Julian had not been unkind, just… unyielding. But she knew that something had been missing, something beyond material comfort. Her 'mother', Joan, had been the one she went to when she felt confused or discouraged, she had been able to relate to her. But why, when Joan had died, had she not deemed it necessary to grieve? Why had she not gone to the funeral? Perhaps because, after Joan told her she was adopted, she no longer felt any responsibility towards them.

Chapter 16

The disappearance of little Johnny Briggs had become a murder inquiry. One day a Panda car parked outside the front gate and a callow-looking uniformed policeman came to the front door. He introduced himself as PC Gale and wanted to know who the owner of the blue van on the driveway was. 'Why? Has the tax expired?' Julian asked flippantly.

'It's to do with the Johnny Briggs case. A blue van was sighted in the vicinity the day before the abduction,' replied the policeman. 'We are checking up on all vehicles of that description in the area.'

'It belongs to my assistant.'

'May I speak to him?'

Julian reluctantly let PC Gale into the hallway and fetched Creighton from the laboratory.

Sitting up in bed, Alana heard voices from below, got up and opened her door. She had become sensitive to the workings of the Mendes House ever since the visit of Jack Goode, as if an air of disquiet had entered with him but had not left when he had. She stood at the top of the stairs and listened.

'Would you mind telling me where you were on the night of April 6th?' Creighton, in a playful mood, tapped his chin and pondered. 'I was here.'

'And the day before?'

'Hmm… that would be the 5th?'

'That's right, sir, the 5th,' agreed the policeman.

Julian had had enough of Creighton's amateur dramatics and cut in. 'That morning you picked up chemical supplies from Cambridge, remember?'

'That's right. I did.'

'And then you spent the rest of the day in the lab with me.'

The policeman seemed puzzled. 'The lab?'

Julian opened the door to the laboratory and let the officer peer inside. 'We do research for the Government.' He shut the door firmly. 'You may verify my work with the authorities. I'll give you a number to call if you like,' Julian said facetiously. PC Gale said that would not be necessary, apologised for the inconvenience and left.

After the policeman had driven away Alana returned to her room. 'But he was out that night, I saw him return with…' She didn't care to entertain anything sinister, but the facts were inescapable. Why had Creighton lied? And why had Julian backed him up?

'You like playing games, don't you?' Julian was in a rage over Creighton's impertinence during the questioning.

'It makes life interesting,' replied his assistant.

'And will you find it interesting when they come and put the handcuffs on?'

'If they come for me…'

Julian scowled. He was becoming increasingly exasperated with Creighton. He had outstayed his usefulness. Maybe it was time to get rid of him, something he should have done years ago.

'You think you are above the law, that your reputation will save you,' Creighton blurted out. 'Well, Professor Hawkes, if I go down… so do you.'

Creighton was coming to the conclusion that if he was going to put his plan into operation, he had better do it soon. His

'Master', he was convinced, was becoming more irrational by the minute. His unconventional working hours, his absentmindedness—he often left the Bunsen burner on allowing chemical samples to dry up—and he was always forgetting where he left his notes. The Professor's appearance also gave reason for concern. In the past Julian's precise, well-groomed look was something he carefully nurtured. His neatly trimmed goatee beard and long golden hair was an important part of the Professor Julian Hawkes public image. But now his hair, turned a greyish white, was straggly, his beard rough and bristly. To Creighton, and no doubt others, he was the personification of the 'mad professor'.

Back in the lab, Julian took the small boy's heart out of the deep freeze and laid it carefully on the bench. He attached two electrodes and turned on the current. He watched closely for signs of life but was disappointed. He then injected a serum into one of the ventricles and increased the flow of electricity. A beat… then another, tiny and irregular but definite proof of life.

'A clean scalpel, quick, from the steriliser,' demanded Julian.

Creighton was loath to obey but eventually opened the unit, retrieved a scalpel, and handed it over. 'Here, Doctor Frankenstein.'

Julian ignored the jibe and began to slice thin sections from the beating heart.

Late that evening, after Creighton had driven away—it was Friday and he had the weekend off—and after Julian had retired, Alana stole downstairs, entered the kitchen, and went out into the garden through the back door. On one of her clandestine visits to the hot house she had found out that there was a spare key to the laboratory hidden in the greenhouse. The mandragora plants displayed their usual affections for her but she managed to tear herself away and, with the key clutched in her hand, let herself in to the lab. She knew that Julian was sometimes careless with certain things and, sure enough, there on the bench next to the steriliser unit was a set of keys. She picked them up and returned to the main part of the house. In the hallway she listened for any signs of life, but all was quiet. As quietly as possible she tried key after key until one fitted and she let herself into Julian's study. What was she looking for? Clues? To what? Perhaps confirmation of the intrigue that she felt was going on? On the desk a large tome was open at a page revealing a crude diagram of a body cut open, its organs separated, laid out and described both in Latin and strange runic symbols. And on the opposite page an image she recognised, a giant mandragora plant. A shudder went through her body. She turned the pages, more grotesque images, strange chemical symbols, astrological charts. The book was entitled Hermaticum Praxis. Her eyes strayed up to the oil painting hanging above the desk, 'The Alchemist'. A realisation came to her. An ugly, unthinkable thought.

She backed out of the study, locked the door and, her curiosity awakened, she returned to the laboratory. The giant mandragora was pleased to see her again and reacted as she approached the chamber. But Alana now had a different view of the plant and edged past on her way to the freezer. Tentatively, afraid of what she might find, she lifted the lid. There, amongst the ice and swirling white mist, were containers with vegetation inside. Also, a plastic box containing what looked like raw meat. She knew that Julian had been experimenting using animal parts and gave them no further thought. She closed the lid and looked around the room. On the bench was a small temperature-controlled observation chamber. Two wires from the unit were connected to a converter plugged into the wall. She leaned over and peered in through the glass. The wires led to two electrodes connected to, what looked like, a small organ, a liver or... a heart. She flicked the switch to 'on'. And when the tissue began to slowly throb... For the briefest moment she was stunned, as if refusing to believe the implication of what was before her. Then came the shock and she stumbled back, knocking over an alembic and it's stand which landed on the floor, the glass smashing. In her distressed and frightened state, she fled the laboratory, forgetting to lock the door behind her. Alana rushed into the garden. In her panic she dropped the bunch of keys on the patio. She was about to enter the house by the kitchen door but hesitated and looked up at the brooding structure, dark against the night sky, the house she had once called home. For the first time in her life a feeling came to her, a mixture of pity and revulsion. She turned and ran away into the darkness.

Julian entered the lab early. He was alarmed to see the broken glass on the floor and the door into the garden wide open. His first thought was 'burglars' and rushed to his study. It was locked. He searched feverishly for the keys, cursing his carelessness, eventually finding them on the patio. As he picked them up, he noticed that the door to the greenhouse was open. Maybe Creighton had come back, under the influence of drink or drugs... but his van wasn't on the drive. Puzzled, he returned to the house and let himself into the study. At first nothing seemed out of place. The safe, on the floor under the desk, was intact. Then he noticed that the Hermaticum Praxis was closed; he had left it open. It dawned on him that, perhaps, Alana... she was the only other person in the house. He climbed the stairs to her bedroom, pushed open the door and entered. Her bed had been slept in, her day clothes were folded over the back of a chair, her shoes on the floor. Her mobile phone was on the bedside table. The corner of a leaflet poked out from under the pillow. Julian reached for it and was alarmed to see that it was for an adoption agency. He tried to contain his mounting hysteria. He ran around the house calling her name, dashed into the garden searching for her. An hour later, after scouring the grounds and surrounding countryside, Julian returned to the Mendes House. He hadn't thought to look in the garage and pulled open the doors to discover Alana's car had gone. For the first time in his life, he felt vulnerable, alone, bereft of solutions.

While Julian was sitting in the kitchen anxiously speculating about what had happened, Alana was driving down the motorway towards London. She had calmed down since her fright and concluded that the only person she could turn to was Maurice. He was not an unreasonable man, was fairly intelligent and he adored her. But then, so was Julian; all those things and more. How could he…? She still hadn't quite correlated the thoughts that ran through her mind. Maybe there was a simple explanation. No, she rejected that idea, but perhaps there was a complicated but rational one. She drove on, arriving outside the Kensington home just after six o'clock.

She had left with no handbag, house keys or phone; she hadn't dared to go back into the house after spending what seemed like an eternity roaming the lanes and fields surrounding the Mendes House. As her panic died down, and she was able to gather her thoughts Alana recalled that she had left the car keys in the ignition and was able to get away unheard and unseen.

She rang the bell and had to wait some time before a bleary-eyed Maurice appeared, wearing bathrobe over his pajamas. He was surprised at first and then pleased but he sensed that something was wrong. He took her into the basement kitchen, made a cup of tea and in the gentlest of tones waited for an explanation. Still trying to sort everything out in her mind, Alana began to describe, in a jumbled sort of way, the events of the past few days. Maurice was patient with her but when, as her description turned to occurrences in Julian's laboratory, a sense of alarm began to take hold of him.

'What do you mean... surely it could have been a rabbit's or a monkey's heart?'

'The night before he had returned late... with a bundle... and took it into the laboratory...' Alana muttered.

'He? Who?'

When she turned to the policeman's visit Maurice broke into a sweat. He dashed off upstairs and returned a few minutes later fully dressed. Alana heard him on the stairs outside the kitchen talking in a low voice on his mobile phone. 'I'm leaving now... yes, see you up there, and Jack, not a word to anyone until we find out what is going on.'

Chapter 17

Creighton had arrived at the Cambridge flat that Friday evening to find Alice asleep in front of the television. An empty bottle of wine was on the table beside her. He had become increasingly worried about her state of mind, and he often stopped off at the pub to fortify himself with a few pints before returning in the hope that she had drunk herself into a stupor. Her mood swings were frequently extreme, from clinging sentimentality to physical violence. He knew that keeping her cooped up in the flat was no longer an option. The previous weekend she had gone out, against his strict instructions and he had to search for her, eventually finding her propping up the bar in 'The George', regaling the locals with stories of her time in Spain... 'What else has she told them?' he wondered as he took her back to the flat.

He looked down at her. Her beauty had faded. Advancing years and the drink and drugs had taken their toll. He covered her with a blanket and made the decision that tomorrow would be his day of reckoning with Professor Julian Hawkes. Hers also. Alice would get her chance to pay back for the years of misery and exploitation, whether she would know it or not.

In times of stress, and they had been few and far between, Julian found consolation in the Hermaticum Praxis. But this morning was different. He felt as if things were happening beyond his control, 'his world' that he had so carefully constructed, was unravelling. He was trying to concentrate on the chapter on

Demonology when he heard the familiar sound of car tyres on the gravel drive outside. Feeling confident that it was Alana returning, and expecting her apology for not telling him where, or why, she had left, he remained in the study.

'Professor Hawkins!' He recognised the odious voice of Maurice's devoted follower and then a terrible thought came to him. In his search for Alana, he had left the front door unlocked. 'Did I do the same with the laboratory door?' He closed the book and dashed out. The hall was empty. He headed straight for the lab. The door was open, and he found Jack peering at the mandrake plant in the chamber. He had his mobile in his right hand and waved it across the glass. It seemed to recoil from him.

'Interested?' ' asked Julian in a way that made it clear he was not bothered about Jack's response.

'Maurice and his wife are on their way.'

Julian ignored this piece of information and adopted a tone of superiority. 'Mandragora Officinarum. It grows around the Mediterranean, Turkey, some species come from the Himalayas.'

Jack moved on around the bench and trod on the broken glass. 'An accident?' he inquired.

'The plant contains hallucinogenic tropane alkaloids, useful in the treatment of psychosis.'

'Where's that assistant of yours? Creighton… isn't that his name?'

'The English Mandrake, Bryonia Alba, has, in the past, been used in pagan rituals.'

Jack stared down at the human heart connected to the electrodes. Maurice had told him what Alana had reported but being a creature who only believed in material things he had dismissed any hint of 'other-worldly' concepts. 'What is it? A monkey? A rabbit?

'You wouldn't understand?'

'Alana seems to think it might be something other than… animal…'

Julian interrupted him. 'We are all animals… of one kind or another.'

'… And what's it got to do with the work you are being paid to carry out?'

Julian, suddenly, had had enough of Mister Jack Goode. 'Get out. If you read my contract, it states that I am to have absolute control over any experiments I carry out… with no questions asked.'

Jack remained, arrogantly standing his ground by the bench. 'You are not dealing with a bumptious, self-seeking, politician anymore, Professor.' He pointed his phone at Julian. 'We are in charge now.' Julian was startled at Jack's sudden change of tone and manner. He was no longer the errand boy, no longer the slavish acolyte.

'We… ?'

'Surprised? An educated man like you shouldn't be. The Foundation had been in charge since the beginning. I was given the task of making sure the Honourable Member stayed on course.'

Julian could only just stare, at the brash young man who had turned into someone to be reckoned with.

'There have been moments when Maurice has become, shall we say, sentimental over certain aspects of the plan. Take that visit to the Special Needs School up north. I advised him against it, but he went ahead, no doubt due to his wife's eloquent methods of persuasion. One day I found him reading an article on-line about how the mentally ill were dealt with by the Third Reich. Afterwards he began to redraw the map on privatisation, excluding the vulnerable and needy from the process.'

For the first time in his life Julian was confronted with someone whose arrogance matched his own and he found it troubling. 'What makes you think Alana has any influence over her husband?'

Jack laughed. 'How little you know of your own daughter. She is the arch manipulator. You may recall the incident at university? A suicide, I believe was the official finding. More like murder by Alana the 'cock-teaser'. Yes, Professor Julian Hawkes, the Bracho Institute knows everything.' His laugh had turned into a sneering indictment.

Julian, beyond fury, was about to launch himself forward and strangle Jack Goode but managed to restrain himself and uttered, through tight lips, 'how little you know of my family.' He was on the point of revealing the   secret of Alana's origins when the sound of a car outside stopped him. He turned and left the laboratory. As he   entered the hall, Maurice, looking rather flustered, appeared. With him was Alana. She had regained her cold,   detached manner. In the drive up from London she had refused to answer any of Maurice's questions; mostly to do with the state of their marriage and how a divorce, at this time, could be damaging to his chances of becoming party leader.

Julian held out his hand and, in a tone less of an invitation, more of a command, said, 'Alana.' He was hoping that she would side with him as his ally. Alana hesitated before moving away from her husband but also away from her stepfather and she took up a position on neutral ground at the foot of the stairs. At this moment Jack came into the hallway. He was finishing a call on his mobile, '… yes, come right away.' He and Maurice exchanged nervous looks. Julian, disappointed at Alana's indifference to his plight, made light of the situation, smiled his winning smile, and said, 'well, here we all are.'

'I want some explanations, Julian.' Maurice spoke with a less than authoritative voice. 'And I don't want any prevarication. I want to know what's going on here.'

Julian was slow to answer. 'What's going on, Maurice? Why, precisely what you… and your Foundation,' he looked over at Jack, '…engaged me to do.'

'Alana… my wife… had been telling me some…' before he could finish Julian turned and marched over to Alana, took her forcefully by the arm and led her into the laboratory. Maurice and Jack followed.

As Alana entered, the Mother Plant stirred and appeared to reach out to her. Maurice, still agitated, stood by the bench. 'I demand to know exactly what experiments have been undertaken.' Jack, standing behind him in the doorway, smiled to himself and shook his head. Julian lifted the window of the observation chamber. He took a scalpel blade from the sterilisation unit, reached into the chamber, and cut off a stem of the mandragora. Alana swooned and grabbed hold of the side of the chamber. Maurice, unable to make the connection, turned to her. 'Darling! Are you all right?'

After a moment she seemed to recover and Maurice, much relieved, was about to make another demand. Julian laid the stem on the bench and cut into it with a vicious thrust of the blade. This time, Alana buckled at the knees and groaned. Jack stepped forward, the smile on his face was gone, a look of horror replaced it.

Maurice looked on with disbelief. He was confused and sweating profusely. Julian stabbed again and again until Alana was on the floor, gasping for breath, the pain coursing through her body.

'You see! You see what I, Professor Julian Hawkes, has created? And I did it for you and for... Bracho.' He threw down the scalpel, rushed over to Alana and helped her up. 'I'm sorry, Alana. But it was the only way to prove to these clods, these 'men in suits', who is the Master here.' Alana glanced at him, a look of bewilderment on her face, and then stumbled out of the lab. She made her way upstairs and into her room where she collapsed onto the bed.

'You crazy bastard,' muttered Jack. Maurice was speechless, still trying to put the pieces together.

'Crazy?' Julian swept back his mop of silver hair. His eyes shone with confidence and bravado. He seemed to have grown inches. He strode over to the human heart and switched on the electrical current. After a few moments the heart began to beat, albeit very faintly. Jack made his way over and looked down at the organ. He was smart enough to put two and two together and come up with four.

'It's what you asked for. A fit and healthy regime. No more weak, enfeebled people. No more a drain on society. My experiments, the work that the Bracho Foundation commissioned, is just beginning to bear fruit.' Julian switched off the current, the heart ceased beating. Jack was fully aware of the implications. He looked over at Maurice, still dithering, still mystified. Jack went over to the deep freeze and lifted the lid. He cast his eye over the contents. He was searching for conclusive evidence. He took out a polythene bag containing mandragora leaves. Then the plastic box with what looked like offal inside. He placed the box on the bench and opened it. Inside were the liver, kidney, brain, spleen of little Johnny Briggs. Maurice had recovered enough of his wits to join Jack and gaze down at the bloody remnants. 'What is it? Rabbit, monkey?'

'You think you've found something, don't you, Jack?' Julian's scorn was obvious.

'What is going on?' demanded an exasperated Maurice. 'Will someone tell me?' He looked from Julian to Jack and back again. Julian took the box from the bench, fastened the lid, and replaced it in the deep freeze. The expression on his face, a broad grimace, was akin to that of someone approaching insanity. Jack was deep in thought, weighing all the evidence as he saw it and wondering how he was going to present the facts to his employers. It was clear to him that both the professor and the politician were not capable of rational thought... at the moment anyway. 'Maurice, you and I need to talk,' and he led him out of the lab and back into the hallway. Julian, sensing that he had achieved some sort of victory, coolly and calmly set about clearing up the broken glass on the floor. It occurred to him that this was a job his assistant, Creighton, should have been doing.

Chapter 18

At roughly the same time as events were unfolding at the Mendes House, Creighton drove the van from Cambridge and into the countryside. Beside him was Alice.

Ever since he had promised that he would find her daughter she had nagged him remorselessly. But now was the time for his sweet revenge. Over breakfast one morning he explained that he had found her, her name was Alana, she was living with a family not too far away and that he had arranged a visit the next weekend. Alice became almost hysterical with excitement. Creighton was stern with her, said she must take her pills but no alcohol. All week she had been very good, had with much difficulty, remained sober, stayed in the flat and spent hours in front of the mirror choosing the right clothes to wear. By the end of the week her whole demeanour had changed. Creighton had gone to the pub on his way home from work and had his customary two pints. On arriving at the flat he was surprised to find Alice all dressed and ready to go. Eventually he persuaded her to go to bed, '… get a few hours, at least,' he urged her. 'You want your daughter to see you looking your best.' However, by the time Creighton awoke, she was bathed and dressed and eager to commence the journey.

On the same morning that Alana was driving up to the Mendes House with her husband, Alice and Creighton were setting off for the same destination in his blue van.

Alana had never cried. She had never learnt to cry. Although her upbringing had been sheltered compared with other children, she had had her fair share of minor accidents, a fall from a horse, a tumble down the stairs, a burn from the Bunsen burner in the laboratory during a science lesson, but she displayed a stoicism that Julian was proud of. As she sat in her room, she remained dry-eyed. She took the adoption leaflet out of the drawer and turned the pages. 'Why can't I feel anything?' she asked herself. 'Why can't I feel anything for others?' Since the incident in the laboratory, she had been attempting to come to terms with her sense of self. Maurice had not helped. He was only concerned with his public image and his ambitious bid for party leadership. 'Why did I ever marry him,' was the question that came to her confused mind. 'Perhaps... to get away from Julian's over-protective presence.' She wasn't sure. Who else could she turn to? Jack Goode? There was something untrustworthy about him. She recalled the moment at the recent Party Conference in Blackpool when, at a late-night party, he had made a pass at her and he wasn't drunk, unlike most of the other revellers. 'How would you like to lose your virginity to a real man,' was his offer. At first, she thought he was joking, then the ugly thought, ... *had Maurice confided to him about their disastrous wedding night?* Then his hand disappeared up her dress and he pressed his mouth on hers. She reacted with the same force that she had adopted with the others who tried to take advantage of her. 'Cock teaser,' was Jack's response as he stumbled back. 'Doesn't anything get through to you?' He walked away. She felt no sense of anger towards him, in fact, she felt sorry for him, as she did for most of the men and boys who had crossed her path. She didn't tell her husband of the incident. 'Why not? Did I not want Jack to lose his job?' Maurice had said that he couldn't have got where he was today without Jack's help. Telling on him would have been a superb act of revenge.

She listened as voices, muted, came up from the hallway. It was Maurice and Jack. They sounded conspiratorial, whispering in desperate tones.

After clearing up the broken glass, Julian had returned to work. It had often been his reaction when in troubling situations to shut out the outside world and get his head down. With a single-minded sense of purpose, he lit the Bunsen burner and began heating up a solution in an alembic. There was something odd about his actions, as if it was stubbornness that was motivating him rather than scientific inquiry. In truth, the events of the last two days had unbalanced the usual orderly pattern of work. Unable to concentrate he decided to consult his 'touchstone', the Hermaticum Praxis. He left the room and strode towards the study.

As he entered the hall, Maurice and Jack halted their discussion and looked up at him with a mixture of guilt and indignation. He hesitated before sweeping past them and unlocking the study door. This was no time to challenge these 'little people' with their trifling conspiracy theories, he told himself. He took up his 'bible', locked the study door and returned to the lab.

It was while he was engrossed in archaic procedures about an hour later that Julian heard voices in the hall. One seemed vaguely familiar. Intrigued, he left his studies and cautiously entered the hall.

Standing by the front door was Creighton, a triumphantly malevolent look on his face. On his arm was Alice. It took her a moment to take in the assembled awkward-looking characters before she recognised Julian. He, in turn, was slow to recognise her, but before he could say or do anything they were all conscious of Alana descending the stairs.

Creighton was relieved that there were others present. The thought of taking on just Julian was not one he relished. Maurice, he remembered seeing, but he wasn't quite sure he had seen the other, younger man before. With a brazen look on his face Creighton shattered the eerie silence. 'Alice... I'd like you to meet your daughter, Alana.'

Alana, still reeling from the events of the past few hours, stopped on the stairs and regarded the woman who stood below her with a mixture of disbelief and fear. Surely this frump, this confused looking woman couldn't be her birth mother.

Alice gazed up at Alana, her heart pumping, her emotions agitated to the point of hysteria. She was also aware of Julian, her old lover, staring at her in disbelief.

Maurice was still trying to come to terms with the 'experiment' that he had witnessed earlier. His head told him that Julian had been playing 'tricks', using superior scientific knowledge to outwit him, but his heart conveyed a completely different story. His politician's instinct for survival told him to leave, to end it, and he stepped forward. 'Julian...' but before he could continue Julian spoke out.

'Alana, go to your room,' he ordered as if she were a child again. But Alana was mesmerized and intrigued and continued down the stairs. Julian transferred his attention to Creighton and was about to launch himself at his cocksure assistant, but Jack anticipated his move and stepped between them. 'Now, Julian. I don't know who these people are but...'

Maurice, by now, even more confused, shook his head and turned away.

'My daughter...' Alice stepped closer to Alana and reached out her hand, but her 'daughter' was not ready for physical contact. Not yet and certainly not with this strange creature.

'Don't be unkind, Alana. After all, a girl's best friend is her mum.' Creighton was beginning to enjoy his 'revenge'.

Alana's fears turned to revulsion. She recoiled, twisted her body, and turned to go back upstairs but Julian was in her way, so she pushed past Alice and rushed out of the hallway down the corridor and into the laboratory.

'You're sick, Hawkes. I'm going to see that you pay for your crimes,' Jack whispered in Julian's ear before taking Maurice by the arm and ushering him out through the front door and towards his car.

Julian looked daggers at Creighton and Alice. 'I should have killed you both myself,' he muttered, an uncharacteristic hint of regret in his voice. Alice shrank back. Creighton had assured her that the reunion would be untroubled. Yes, there would be much to discuss and many things to come to terms with but nothing that could not be arrived at satisfactorily for all parties. What had gone wrong? Why had her daughter rejected her?

Alana stumbled in a confused state around the laboratory until she came up against the observation chamber. The Mother Plant responded and stretched out towards her. In an instinctive move, she lifted the glass door. The green tendrils reached out and enveloped her, mingled with her hair, curled round her limbs. 'Surely,' she asked herself, 'my...' But she couldn't elaborate— it all seemed too fantastic. She stared down at the slivers of plant on the bench. She reached out and grasped the scalpel that, earlier, her father had been wielding. In another instinctive gesture she stabbed the scalpel into one of the main stems of the mother plant. A piercing scream filled the room. Alana staggered; a jolt of pain coursed through her body. She dropped the scalpel and tore herself from the clinging tendrils. As she blundered away, the terrible truth came to her.

She was a product of her father's devilish experiments, of his fiendish ambitions. And another terrifying thought flashed through her confused mind, *was she only part-human?* As if to confirm her worst fears the Mother Plant was in the process of moving out of its 'prison' and began to glide awkwardly along the bench towards her. Was this an attempt to reconnect or an act of revenge?

Alana shrank back, knocking to the floor the alembic containing the opaque liquid and sending the Bunsen burner, which Julian had left unattended, skidding into the 'Hermaticum Praxis'. The old dry pages immediately caught fire and soon spread to a pile of medical papers and a discarded lab coat.

Julian burst in and was horrified to see the chaos that was ensuing. His first thought was to save the 'Hermaticum Praxis' and he dashed forward, knocked it away from the flames and into a sink. He turned on the tap. By this time the plant was moving at a sustained rate. Julian recovered the Bunsen burner and used the naked flame to check the advancing Mandrake. The plant screamed as it was scorched by his thrusting gestures. Alana flinched in agony with every hurt that was inflicted. She fell to the floor where her hand alighted on the discarded scalpel. Julian continued to assault the plant until its leaves were singed and began to burn. 'I created you and I will destroy you,' he uttered.

His actions were brought to a halt by a sudden pain in his back. Alana withdrew the blade and, as he turned to face her, she stabbed again, downward into his chest. The blade broke off. He dropped the burner and, with a look of disbelief on his face, sank to the floor. The expression on his creation's face was one of incredulity, as if unable to comprehend her own actions. Had she mistaken Julian for another, Jack Goode perhaps, or her husband? Or was she protecting her own flesh and blood?

Outside, in the greenhouse, the massed ranks of Mandrake plants, sensing that their survival was under threat, had become agitated. Their first instinct was to save the Mother Plant. They swayed and swirled; tendrils began to lash out. The glass panels began to break, the aluminium structure twisted and arched under the pressure from the surge.

Seeing smoke billowing along the corridor from the laboratory, Creighton hustled Alice out of the hall and into the front yard where they joined Maurice and Jack. She was beside herself with grief and torment and staggered off, head in hands, tears streaming, her make-up running down her face creating a grotesque mask. Creighton turned, saw the flames coming from the laboratory and dashed around to the side of the house.

His strategy for vengeance had not gone to plan. But then he thought, maybe the outcome was going to be even more than he had hoped for. As he rounded the side of the house, he was aware of the sound of breaking glass. He stopped in his tracks, confronted by an army of Mandrake plants attempting to escape from the greenhouse.

As he came alongside the open laboratory door, he was aware of a figure in the doorway of the burning room. Alana, coughing and gasping for air, had managed to make her way towards the door but had then flagged, unable to continue. In a moment of spontaneity, Creighton grabbed her and pulled her to safety. She staggered to her feet and pushed her rescuer away. A sudden dilemma arose within her. Should she endure as human or plant? Where did her allegiances lie? She was drawn to both and seemed unable to move, the flames at her back, the Mandrake plants before her.

The primitive instinct in the plants was matched by

Creighton's. After all, his crazed mind reasoned, he was the one who had fed and nurtured the plants from seed. They were 'his' creation. He rushed forward and attempted to shut the door and contain the plants. 'They won't hurt me!' The glass in the door shattered in his face, he staggered back, blood pouring from his wounds, fell to the floor and was trampled to death by the remorseless advance of the ungrateful horde.

Julian Hawkes, lying prone on the laboratory floor was not finished. His prodigious will, the driving force that had brought him this far, compelled him to cling to life, whatever the cost. His clothes were soaked with blood, but he staggered towards the door, his half-burnt, half-soaked 'bible' in his grasp. A scream from behind caused him to turn. The Mother Plant, by now a tower of flame, advanced towards him in its bid to reach its 'offspring'. Alana also heard the scream and, turning towards the source, re-entered the laboratory. In a cataclysm of conflagration, Stepfather, Mother and Daughter finally came together and finally perished together.

Maurice and Jack watched helplessly as the fire spread from the ground floor into the remainder of the house. Jack was pleased at the devastating speed of the blaze but, anxious to make sure that all was consumed, he ran across to the side of the house where he witnessed the incineration of the Mandrake plants and the last moments of Julian and Alana, ablaze in the burning laboratory. *How fitting,* he thought and rushed back to the front of the house.

After the initial shock had subsided, Maurice's concern was for his standing as an elected public servant once news got out regarding the fire at Professor Hawkes residence. Only after realising that nothing incriminating was likely to be found once the flames had died down, a fact confirmed emphatically by Jack, did his thoughts turn to the whereabouts of his wife. He instantly assumed the emotions suitable for that of a distressed husband. Jack was surprised but not fooled by Maurice's outburst and made a show of comforting the grieving politician. Neither acknowledged Alice, the only other living person present, sobbing uncontrollably as her world crashed around her.

A large shiny black car drew up outside the gate and Gordon MacDonald leapt out. He joined Maurice and Jack on the gravel drive.

'What do we know?' he asked in his customary bureaucratic tone.

Maurice was too distressed to answer. Jack came to his aid. 'Hawkes out of control. Gone mad. Set the place alight rather than reveal anything to us. But don't worry. I doubt if any evidence will be left afterwards.'

'Has anyone called the fire brigade?'

'Not yet, as far as I know.'

The man from the Treasury Department took out his mobile phone and called the emergency services. As he did so he turned his back on the burning house and as he relayed the information to a CAD operator, he noticed a bedraggled woman staggering forlornly away down the lane.

He ended the call and turned to Jack. 'Better get Maurice back to London before the police arrive. Make sure everything, and I mean everything, is destroyed. I'll take care of any Treasury business and I trust you will do the same for Bracho?'

Jack nodded and took Maurice by the arm. 'It's useless, Maurice. No one could survive in there.' Maurice buried his face in his hands.

'His wife, too?' said MacDonald. Jack nodded again and led the distraught politician to his car.

Gordon MacDonald, ever the practical man, was already drafting his official version of events. 'Professor Julian Hawkes, engaged in research work for the Ministry of Health died in an accidental fire at his home in Cambridgeshire, etc, etc...' But his mind uncharacteristically wandered into speculation regarding the nature of what really went on at the Mendes House.

By now the Mendes House was an inferno, the flames reaching up high into the night sky. In the first moments of the blaze, some of the leaves of the Hermaticum Praxis had burst from their binding as the heat intensified. A few were borne out, soared away, and landed on the gravel of the front yard. One page, scorched at the edges, caught Gordon MacDonald's eye and he bent over and picked it up. The writing was in an obscure script, but with the help of the flickering light from the burning house he was able to make out the words of what seemed to be a poem.

'Go and catch a falling star, Get with child a mandrake root, Tell me where all past years are, Or who cleft the devil's foot...'

THE END